I0691379

THE DARK SIDE

A story of commitment, a life of service.

First Edition

Published by The Nazca Plains Corporation
Las Vegas, Nevada
2010

ISBN: 978-1-935509-86-8

Published by

The Nazca Plains Corporation ®
4640 Paradise Rd, Suite 141
Las Vegas NV 89109-8000

PUBLISHER'S NOTE
The Dark Side is a work of fiction created wholly by *Pavel Servus'* imagination. All characters are fictional and any resemblance to any persons living or deceased is purely by accident. No portion of this book reflects any real person or events.

Male Cover Photo
aFOTOMarkowskaMagolon

Art Director
Blake Stephens

DEDICATION

The story is dedicated to Peter, Mark and Ian, also Wayne, Kel, Tom, Steve, Rob (all three of you) and the many, many slaves and Masters who have helped the author realize more than a few dreams.

THE DARK SIDE

A story of commitment, a life of service.

First Edition

Pavel Servus

PART 1

After ten years of trawling leather bars, answering ads in the gay press and spreading your profile far and wide on the internet, you were about to give up on the whole BDSM scene. Between the no-shows, the cyber-wankers and the absolute liars, it seemed there was nobody interested in real BDSM, the long-term master-slave life style or indeed, any serious bondage or S & M play. As a committed slave you were seeking a life serving other men, sexually and otherwise, not as a one-night stand or a weekend job, but as a serious, long-term commitment. You did not imagine completely sacrificing your career, but imagined it quite possible to be a slave and serve a Master, at the same time progressing with a professional life. When not physically serving a master, you imagined being mentally committed to him, and locked in some adornment of servitude, possibly a chastity device, the key to which was held only by the Master. This seemed an impossible goal, until you stumbled across Master Peter, a friend of a friend, who contacted you by email one day.

You had been corresponding with Master Peter now for the last four weeks, via the internet. He told you he was a successful stockbroker with a large house in the city and one in the country and he had sent you photos of the town house with its high wall. The country house was on 20 acres and surrounded by dense forest. He did not tell you anything about his private life but you had heard from a friend, who was also a slave, that he regularly held leather/rubber/bondage parties at his house in the country and that only a few wealthy people were ever invited. You wondered if Master Peter was the same man you had seen giving seminars on Investing in the city; a powerfully built, tall man, immaculately dressed and with rough, handsome features. He passed you the occasional glance and smile, that immediately suggested he would like to know you better. You had heard some gossip that he was a very private man, with few friends.

Over the previous four weeks the Master had explained exactly what he wanted you to do. Each message made you more and more excited so now, one day before you were to travel to the city, you could think of nothing other than the long weekend ahead with Master Peter. Each time you received a message from him, short and abrupt though it was, you immediately got a hard-on. For the last week you had not been able to concentrate on your work as an accountant. Your boss had reprimanded you for making mistakes, daydreaming and forgetting to submit reports. Even though you had never met him, you could not get the image of Master Peter out of your mind.

The instructions were perfectly clear. Catch the 3.45 pm train to the city and wait by the kiosk in the railway station. Wear jeans, white sweatshirt, boots and carry a small, blue case containing toothbrush and essential toiletries only. You will not need spare clothes.

Master Peter also explained what you had to do in preparation for the meeting. For four days before the weekend you were to eat nothing, only drink high protein, high energy drinks. You noticed that you stopped shitting two days before the weekend, but you continued to pass lots of piss. The day of your travel you were to give yourself three consecutive enemas with warm water. This made sure you were completely cleaned out and empty. The last enema was two hours before your were to go to the train station, so you were able to squeeze every last drop of fluid out before you prepared for the next stage. You already owned black rubber shorts, with attached medium sized, black, rubber butt plug, with a hole at the front for your cock and balls to come through. You greased up the butt plug and slipped the shorts on, pulling your cock and balls through the hole. The plug, as always, felt good sliding around in your arse whenever you moved. Master Peter instructed you to screw on a heavy metal ball ring that pulled your balls severely down into the sac. This ring was three cm deep and it was only by pulling the balls down first with a parachute that you managed to get the ring on. As you tightened the key, the ring pulled your balls deep into the sac and swung around when ever you moved. You felt the metal loop at the back of the ring to enable the attachment of further weights or anchors. It felt great.

Master said you could dress in the jeans, sweat shirt and boots and although it was uncomfortable to bend over to get the boots on, you knew this would be nothing compared to sitting for two hours on the train with the butt plug jammed up your arse and the ball ring bulging in front of your jeans. The bulge attracted the attention of some passengers but you ignored them, secretly enjoying being so exposed. You enjoyed the periodic bumping of the train that forced the butt plug further into your arse, but after an hour it started to become uncomfortable. You tried to remain still because there was no way to get the plug out, unless you stripped off in the train. You resigned yourself to suffer, remembering what Master Peter said – any deviation from the instructions and the meeting would be cancelled. You wondered if the pain was showing on your face and if other passengers realized what lie beneath your tight jeans. After two hours you decided to stand in the corridor, to relieve the pressure from the plug in your arse and from the ring on your balls, but by now you were rock hard and had to move your erect cock to one side in your jeans to relieve the pressure. You wondered if you could walk normally because of the pressure in your arse, your balls and now on your cock, but a short walk along the corridor did not attract attention.

Now, committed to the event, you looked forward to your meeting with Master Peter, and all that would happen. As the train drew into the city station your excitement rose. Your heart pounded as you walked the length of the platform, remembering how all this had come about and wondering if this was all a big mistake and whether you should just get on the train back home. You thought you might be found naked, bound and gagged in some backstreet, and then have to explain to the police how you came to be in that situation. Too late to back out now, you thought as you waited by the kiosk at the end of the platform. You were perspiring slightly, even though it was cold outside. The smell from the rubber shorts rose up and immediately excited you. You squirmed with excitement and anticipation.

'Stand still slave and stop looking around at everyone,' you hear from behind you.

Turning slightly, you see Master Peter. You recognize him from the seminar, although now, dressed in a leather jacket and cap with faded tight jeans and boots, he looks even more handsome.

'Don't look at me slave, look at my feet,' growls Master.

You turn your eyes down to stare at his boots, which were high heeled, knee length motorbike boots, worn outside his jeans. As your eyes were travelling down his legs you noticed the outline of handcuffs in his pocket.

'Sorry,' you mumble.

'Sorry what, shit-head,' he says in a low, threatening voice.

'Sorry Sir,' you reply, being sure he heard you without shouting. You knew from previous Masters that they hate having to remind you about slave etiquette.

'Walk ahead of me and out the door. Go over to the black van in the corner of the car park. Don't run and don't dawdle.'

Slowly but deliberately you make you way out of the station and into the car park. You hear his boots on the ground behind you; a heavy, menacing step. At the side of the van and still looking down at the ground you see Master Peter's hand come round you and open the door.

'Get inside the back, face backwards and sit on the floor. Don't move.'

Inside the van you sit and grimace as the butt plug is forced, once again, deep into your arse and your balls crushed by the ring. You know to keep your hands behind you. Master Peter gets into the drivers seat and the van slowly pulls out of the station.

Because the windows of the van are darkened you have no idea what direction you are heading. After 10 minutes he pulls over, stops the van and gets in the back via the side door. You smell his leather jacket and see his shadow as he moves behind you.

'OK slave, clothes off, apart from your shorts, and remember to look at the floor all the time.'

You undress slowly, folding your clothes and stacking them neatly in the corner. You hear him rummaging around in a trunk and the clanking of chains. Standing only in your rubber shorts he pushes you to your knees on the floor. Still looking at the floor your hands are roughly pulled behind your back and you hear and feel the ratchet of handcuffs as they grip your wrists. With your palms facing outwards there is no way to feel the connecting hinge, but you notice the cuffs are semi-rigid and only hinge one way. You hear two clicks as the cuffs are locked, preventing them from tightening as you move your hands; the signs of an experienced and thoughtful Master you think. Quickly, and without ceremony, a leather hood is pulled over your head and neck. You notice there are no eyeholes but there is a mouth hole, which tightly encircles your lips. The hood is tightly fitting but additional straps enable the Master to pull it even tighter around your head. It fits snugly around your neck, and he adjusts the attached collar. The collar is pulled tight and locked with a padlock. You feel the weight of the padlock when the Master lets go. A bit gag is strapped in tightly, so that the corners of your mouth are stretched painfully. Although the bit gag is immovable, you are grateful for it because you are afraid of carsickness, and had the Master inserted a ball gag or dick gag and you had vomited, that could have been fatal. Another sign of a thoughtful Master, you note. The Master attaches a chain to the cuffs and around the padlock on your collar, and then cruelly pulls your wrists up your back, causing you to bend your head and neck backwards.

Hands cuffed and hood locked in place, the Master turns his attention to your feet. You feel heavy metal manacles being locked around your ankles and a short connecting chain prevents any movement. Master then attaches a chain to the ball ring anchor loop via a small padlock then lowers you to the floor on your front. Your head is pulled backwards because of the chain to the cuffs, but you notice that you can breathe OK, although talking is just a mumble. Master pulls the chain from the ball ring, around your ankle manacles, then pulls it tightly and attaches it via another padlock to your cuffs. The result is a tight hog position and any movement pulls on your collar and threatens to pull your balls off.

Meantime your cock is rock hard and crushed beneath your belly, and the butt plug remains a constant reminder that Master has thought to leave no hole open.

The next thing you hear is a chain rattling, then your cuffed hands are lifted up as the chain tightens. You presume the chain passes through a beam in the roof of the van. This puts extra pressure on your collar and your balls feel as though they are about to be ripped off. Completely immobile, Master asks if you are OK. Not withstanding the excruciating pain in your neck and balls, you are in slave heaven. You mutter 'yes Sir' into your bit gag, which comes out accompanied by a shower of spittle. You have dreamt of this type of bondage for ages – tight, painful, gagged, hooded, being taken to some unknown place, for abuse by some unknown person or persons. You are afraid yet very aroused and, as you try to masturbate against the van floor, every movement sends shudders of pain through your tightly bound body.

The van moves off again, winding and weaving and, after half an hour, bumps up a dirt road. At least being anchored to the roof of the van prevents any sliding around in the van, but every bump puts extra strain on your neck and balls through the hog position and chains. You don't get carsick but you do a lot a dribbling onto the van floor, praying that the Master is not pissed off about this.

Eventually the van comes to a stop. You presume it's now late afternoon and when the van door opens, a rush of cool air confirms this. Master unchains you from the roof and releases your legs. He helps you stand up and step out of the van, but because your wrists are still painfully drawn up to your neck and your ankle manacle has only a short connecting chain, you are very unsteady. Master's strong arms encircle you to steady your movement and slowly he leads you away from the van. You feel dirt under your feet and smell damp leaves and flower scent and presume you are in the forest. The cool air is welcome but you are still sweating inside the tight fitting hood and you feel the sweat dripping out from inside your rubber shorts.

'Stand still,' he commands.

Master unlocks the ankle manacles and kicks your legs apart. You feel pressure on your balls as Master attaches a chain to the ball ring. Your knees fold and you kneel on the ground as he locks the ball chain to some fixture on the ground. Any attempt to stand up is met with shooting pain in your balls, so you stay still, on your knees, with legs apart and balls firmly anchored to the ground.

The next thing your hear is the sound of Masters footsteps disappearing into the distance, a door opening, then closing, then nothing but the birds and wind in the trees. You try to relieve the pressure around your neck but your hands are pulled up tightly to your neck. The cuffs, although loose, are causing pressure on your wrists but no amount of writhing relieves the pain. Any movement is met by searing pain in your balls but all the time your have a rock hard erection with precum oozing from the tip. You are desperate to masturbate but fear for your balls if you move an inch.

Time passes and the air cools. You presume it is now dark. After what seems like two hours, but is probably only 30 minutes, you hear footsteps approaching.

'OK boy, time to set the scene. You came here willingly and you will come to no permanent harm.'

Permanent! What's he talking about. You had not reckoned on coming to any harm, permanent or otherwise. The tight bit gag prevents you speaking but you utter a grunt, which means nothing but resignation to your situation.

'I'm going to take everything off now, but your hands will remain cuffed and the ball ring will remain locked in place. If you decide to bolt, think about a night in the forest, handcuffed, with bears and wolves around and numerous swamps and old mine shafts. It's unlikely you would survive until the morning, but feel free to try if you want.'

Nothing could be further from your mind. Although Master has introduced an element of uncertainty, you are still in bondage heaven.

Slowly Master removes the gag, hood and your shorts. The butt plug plops out followed by a little gas, but no fluid. It takes you a minute to focus in the dim light and to feel steady after being hog tied, then anchored to the ground by your balls, with legs splayed to the side. You work your jaw around to get some mobility into your mouth, after the bit gag forced it open for so long. The cool air bathes your face and crotch and the sweat rapidly dries.

'Here's the situation. You are my slave for the weekend. At all times you will be bound or chained. You will submit to whatever I decide to do or I invite my friends to do. Be sure you will be abused, fucked and forced orally. When not gagged you will answer 'yes Sir' or 'no Sir'. You will cast your eyes down when not blindfolded or hooded, which will not be for long anyway. If you want to be released you can make three jerking movements, or nods of your head. I will immediately release you, but you will be discharged at the same time and sent home. Any questions?'

Your mind is spinning. Is this more than you can cope with, you wonder? You've been looking forward to this for so long; it's your every fantasy and now it's real. You have to go through with it. You cock remains stiffly to attention, confirming your excitement.

'No Sir,' you reply softly.

'Right, get into the house.'

Only now you see the outline of the small house in the trees. A dim light illuminates the interior. Master gives you a few shoves in the back and you walk to the house.

Inside, the dim light shows a fully equipped dungeon with St Andrews Cross, bondage table, beams with hanging chains, a wall festooned with anchor points and an array of hoods, gags, cuffs, restraints, whips, metal spreaders, tit clamps and ball stretchers. Numerous cupboards are closed but you imagine they are full of bondage gear and other torture equipment.

Hands still cuffed, Master leads you to the shower and gives you a hot scrub all over. With your own toothbrush he gently brushes your teeth. His hands caress your body as he covers you with a thin layer of aromatic oil, being sure to apply some to your arse and around your balls. Master allows you to drink some water.

Back in the main room you notice the dining table with a small stool in the middle and strong rings attached to each corner of the table. Your eyes are riveted to the butt plug attached to the stool, larger than anything you have ever experienced. It's made of three lobes of increasing size towards the base, but the base itself is quite narrow. That will ensure it will not be coming out it in a hurry.

Master pushes you onto the bondage table, face up, and ties your feet, knees, thighs, belly, chest and neck to it. Your hands are still cuffed behind you, but Master pushes a pillow into the small of your back to prevent the cuffs pressing on your spine. You think, again, here's a Master who knows what he is doing. The ropes are firm but not tight and you suspect this is only a temporary arrangement.

Your attention follows Master who is getting tubes and gear from a cupboard. Master waves a catheter in front of your eyes and you shudder at the sight. Master says nothing. He puts on sterile gloves, grabs your now flaccid cock and washes it with a blue solution. Next he jams a tube against the cock opening and squeezes in some jelly, which feels cool but is not uncomfortable. After a few minutes your cock goes numb. Catheter in one hand and cock in the other, Master feeds the catheter into your cock until it disappears almost up to the hilt. A sharp, stabbing pains accompanies the final passage of the catheter but this soon subsides. You utter a shriek, but immediately regret it as Master whacks you across the legs with his hand. Master injects some fluid into the catheter and then pulls back slightly to ensure the catheter is lodged firmly in your bladder. Urine flows from the end of the catheter, which Master then clamps. By this time your erection returns and your cock slides up over the catheter. The more you look at it, the more aroused you become.

Next, Master turns his attention to your head. He covers two small flexible tubes with jelly and inserts one into each nostril. They fill your nose and you feel the ends at the back of your nose. You hear your breath coming freely through the tubes. The free ends of the tubes stick out about 5 cm and Master applies tape around your nostrils to make sure they do not fall out.

Master produces a longer, thinner tube and once again covers it with jelly.

'Open you mouth and swallow the tube,' he commands and you obey.

Slowly you feel the tube enter the back of your throat. Master gives you some water and as you swallow he pushes the tubes down into your stomach. There is no discomfort and Master is obviously an expert at this. When the tube is all the way down he tapes the free end to the side of your face.

Master releases all the bonds and forces you to sit on a chair. You obey, realizing that you are slowly loosing control of all your bodily functions. Master controls your piss, your breathing, your mouth and almost certainly will soon control your arse.

You sit there meekly, hands cuffed behind you, tubed and catheterized. You are aroused by the smell of rubber as Master comes from behind you with a black rubber hood. Before he pushes it over your head you notice the wide collar and padlock hanging from the back. Because of the oil, Master has no trouble pulling the hood over and massaging it to fit the contours or your face and neck. There are no eyeholes but the mouth and nose holes are open. You feel Master tighten the wide neck collar and secure the back with the padlock. He pulls the nose and mouth tubes through the holes, applying further tape to the tubes to ensure they will not pull out.

You are able to open your mouth and on command, you open it while Master inserts a wide O-ring, keeping it open. The O-ring is secured by straps to the back of your head. Next you feel a rubber expandable gag being forced into your mouth and fixed behind your head. As the gag is pumped up, all chances of breathing through your mouth are extinguished. Your breath comes easily though the nose tubes so you are not worried. Since you have not eaten you are not worried about vomiting.

You feel Master undoing your handcuffs and soon you are able to rub some life into your wrists. After further scratching around Master, who has said very little, tells you to step into a rubber suit. He guides your feet into the suit, which he then pulls up over your belly and chest and pushes your arms down into the sleeves. You feel rubber gloves and you fiddle your fingers into the rubber tubes. There appear to be holes at the front and back, through which Master pulls your cock and balls and you suspect the nipples and arse are also free. Master zips up the back and zips the top to the rubber collar of your hood. You hear the creaking of leather as Master stoops to padlock metal cuffs around your ankles. The smell of rubber rises into the nose tubes as your body starts to sweat inside the suit.

Your arms are pulled behind your back again, but this time rope is used to secure your wrists and lower arms. Starting at the wrists he draws your arms tightly back, tying your lower arms together so that there is no space between them. The result is that your elbows are pulled back and touching, thereby thrusting your chest and nipples forward. From your elbows he ties rope to the back of your collar and pulls down so that your head is forced backwards.

Without warning Master pushes you forward to the table and forces your head down. A clamp secures your neck to the table. He then kicks your legs apart and ties your ankles to the legs of the table, so that your arse is completely exposed. At the front, your catheterized cock and ring-weighted balls hang down. The next you feel oil being forced into your arse and then one, two, three, four fingers being inserted and moved up and down. You buck and struggle and try to scream but all that comes out is a grunt. Master holds his fingers in your arse for two minutes, as the pain slowly subsides. As you struggle your balls swing around, adding to the pain caused by the heavy metal ring.

Master releases you from the table then by a series of short commands gets you up onto the table and poised, kneeling over the butt plug fixed to the low stool in the middle. You are breathing heavily and your breath makes a whistling noise as it passes through the nose tubes. You anticipate what its to come and wonder if you can take any more.

Well, it's almost too late to worry as the next thing you notice is the strong smell of amyl and you realize Master is holding a swab soaked in amyl over the nose tubes. Soon your head starts to swim but you feel Master's strong arms steadying you. As you sink under the influence of the amyl Master guides your arse onto the butt plug. You are so doped you hardly notice as the tip enters your arse and expands to swallow the first bulge. A further hit of amyl and the second bulge is sucked up into your arse. Master holds you there for a minute as the effects of the amyl wear off. As you come round you notice that the plug is quite flexible, but you still fear the final bulge, which seems huge compared to anything else you have ever tried. Is it time to call it quits? You think, shall I give the release signal? Before your mind clears completely you smell more amyl and you drift away again.

Gently, but firmly, Master forces you down onto the butt plug. You groan inwardly as your arse expands to accommodate the huge bulge. When you are sure that your arse is about to split, the pain reduces and, through your foggy mind, you realize you are over the final bulge and that your arse is clamping over the base of the plug. Slowly you lower yourself further until your buttocks rest on the stool. Although the pain is less, you feel the huge plug up your arse and realize you are fixed to the table, legs splayed to the side, and there is no way you can get the plug out.

Sweat is trickling down your back and out the hole at the bottom and you feel rivulets running down your hood into the body suit. Slowly your breathing comes back to normal and you are relieved that the nose tubes work well, even when you are forced to endure pain.

Your balls are pulled forward and you feel a chain being attached to the ring and padlocked to the table. Now you really are fixed to the table. Your feet are then pulled further outwards and attached to the corners of the table by chains from your manacled ankles to the rings. At this stage your upper body is still free and you try to get comfortable but moving slightly one way and another. Soon, however, you feel chains being threaded through the padlock at the back of your collar and your neck pulled upwards as Master attaches the chains to beams in the ceiling. Now you can neither move your head to the right or left.

You suddenly gasp and let out a muffled scream as two nipple clamps are attached. They are connected by a heavy chain, and the pain is intense when Master lets go of it. You try to lean forward to relieve the pain but the chain attached to your neck collar prevents this. As you struggle the nipple chain swings, adding to the pain. Some further movements and Master attaches a tube from the open end of the catheter to the tube going into your stomach. As he releases the clamp you feel the relief as your bladder empties, sending the urine directly to your stomach for recycling.

So there you sit, encased in rubber, blinded by a hood, gagged with your jaws wide apart, nipples clamped, hands bound tightly behind you, balls stretched, butt plugged, legs pulled apart, catheterized, nose tubed and with a tube going from your cock to your stomach. You are totally immobile, exposed and without control of your bodily functions. Your erection attests to your excitement.

'That's you fixed up for a while,' says Master, and you hear him disappear into the next room.

The pain in your arse, the pain in your neck, the pain in your nipples, the pain in your balls and the aching in your tightly bound arms … you wonder what else Master can inflict on you. You try to relax. Slowly the pain in your arse become tolerable, if you don't move. Similarly the pain in your balls from the padlocked and anchored ball ring eases and your nipples become numb, if you stay perfectly immobile. The only thing you can do is to remain absolutely still. You develop some cramp in your widely spread legs but this passes as you sit lower on the plug.

Your mind wanders back to bondage situations you have had in the past. Mostly they have been temporary, loose affairs from which it has been easy to escape. Masters have promised inescapable bondage but all they've wanted to do is tie you up and gag you so that they can fuck you, then dump you. Master Peter seems severe but experienced and, although your bound, plugged and catheterized entombment in rubber seems extreme, you are aroused like never before. Your erect cock pulls against the ball ring confirming this. Shit, you'd give anything to jerk-off now.

You hear a door open and movements. Straining to identify what's going on you hear what sounds like plates and cutlery being placed on the table. You remember you are in the middle of the table and Master places dinner stuff all around you. At the same time you smell cooking and the aromas make your stomach rumble, remembering that you have not eaten for several days.

After what seems like a short time your hear motorbikes and the sounds of people laughing and joking. The house, which is really only a shack, vibrates as they walk around. You feel them close to you, making comments and tweaking your nipples and cock, making you shudder with pain. You estimate there are three others and guess that they are here to take part in the fun, because they all seem very much at home in Master Peter's house. You hear cans opening and guess they are drinking beer. The laughing gets louder and after a further hour you feel vibrations at the table as they sit down, surrounding you.

Master serves a meal and they all take their time eating and drinking. They comment on how Master has prepared a beautiful centre arrangement for the table, namely you, and occasionally someone tests you by prodding you in the buttocks or cock with a fork. The rubber protects you from serious damage but on one occasion Master gently reprimands a friend for interfering with the ornament.

During the meal you sweat profusely and it drips from the holes around your cock and arse. As the meal ends Master disconnects your stomach tube and pours in more water. He then reconnects the catheter. Throughout, your cock is rigid as you imagine yourself presented in this way, surrounded by men who, it seems, have not just come here for a meal. Your mind runs wild imagining what could be next in store for you.

PART 2

Eventually you smell coffee, and as Master and his guests laugh and joke, you hear plates being removed from the table, chairs being scraped back on the wooden floor and someone wiping the food waste from the table. You feel Master get up on to the table.

'You've been a good ornament boy. Now you will entertain us a while.'

Entertain! What the hell does that mean, you gasp to yourself?

Master releases your chained feet from the corners of the table and the chain holding your neck to the ceiling. With relief you sink onto the low stool, but not far because the butt plug is forced further into your arse. You notice Master leaves the chains dangling from your ankles and neck and when he releases your ball ring, that chain is left attached also.

You feel Master grab your hooded head and smell amyl once again. As your drift away Master lifts you off the butt plug, but you buck and struggle to start with as the widest bulge tears at your already stretched arse. The other two bulges come out easily and you sigh with relieve at being free from the monstrous plug. You wonder if Master will also release your arms, but they remain tightly bound behind your back and tied to your collar.

Master pushes you forward and gently lowers you onto the table, front down. He pulls you to the edge of the table so that your neck is over the edge. Next you feel your ankles being reattached to the corners of the table and further chains attached to your knees and pulled sideways, thereby opening up your arse. The neck chain is attached to the other two corners of the table so that you are fixed, once again, to the table. Master pushes a pillow under your pelvis so that your arse is raised up and gaping. Your balls are trapped painfully by the pillow so Master pulls them backwards. As your cock enlarges however, it pushes into the pillow and is unable to reach its fully erect position. The catheter remains attached to your stomach tube and is adjusted so that it is not kinked.

You feel Master releasing the air from the gag and undo the straps, which hold it in place. He removes the gag but your mouth remains wide open because of the O-ring. You are relieved to take some cool breaths through your mouth, but spit dribbles out as you are unable to swallow. The stomach tube remains stuck in your mouth but you hardly feel it. You feel your head pulled back as Master attaches a chain from the top of your hood to your bound arms. Although your mouth is wide open Master does not remove the nose tubes, which remain firmly fixed in place.

So there you lie, covered in rubber, bound to the table by your ankles and neck, your arse exposed and your mouth wide open. You have never been so exposed and vulnerable. You hear footsteps draw closer and someone gets up onto the table. Cool lubricant is massaged into your arse and two, three, four fingers enter, without resistance, because of the hours you spent on the butt plug.

You hear the ripping of condom packets and resign yourself to getting fucked. This will not be the first time you have been fucked, although in the past you have always had some control over who is fucking you and how they do it. Now you are just a hole. The condom covered cock slides into your arse and the assailant gently works himself in and out. When he thrusts you gasp. His cock must be larger that the butt plug because it hurts like hell. On the second thrust your gasp is cut short by a second condom covered cock jammed suddenly into your mouth. You gag as it touches the back of your throat but no amount of moving can dislodge it. Your head is fixed by the neck chain and chain holding it backwards, so you have no choice but to take it all in.

Being fucked at both ends has always been a fantasy of yours but you always imagined you would have some control, be able to communicate and terminate it when it got too uncomfortable. Now all you can do is lie there and accept your fate, the fate of a bound and abused slave boy. The men fucking you are goaded by the others who encourage deeper penetration and faster thrusting. You feel tears come to your eyes but they run silently down your face inside the rubber hood. You lie there, bucking and twisting, as the men plough away and eventually you gasp as they plunge deeper during what you presume is their orgasm. Slowly they massage their cocks out of your arse and mouth.

Your relief is short lived because, without warning, two more cocks replace those which have just shot their loads. These cocks seem slightly smaller but they are thrust deeply and more rapidly than before. The man at your face grabs your head so that he can thrust his cock deeper, whilst the man at your arse grabs your hips. On and on they go, in, out, in, out, to the cheers of the others. The cock in your arse quickly releases its load and is replaced by yet another cock.

The third cock to fuck your arse is huge, both wider and longer than the others. You suspect this cock is that of Master Peter, because he enters slowly and gently, unlike the others, which were just forced in. Master rests his cock in your arse and lets you relax and feel the pleasure of it right up inside you. Slowly he fucks away but, unlike the others, it is not painful. You groan with delight at the thought and feeling of that huge thing inside you, and of being publicly fucked in this way. Meanwhile the cock at your face finishes its business and leaves your mouth open and dribbling. You groan with pleasure as Master plunges away, his thrusts becoming faster and faster until he explodes with a shout and you feel the warm cum filling his condom.

As Master gets off the table he wipes your arse with a cloth. Gently he caresses your head before leaving you alone. After a while you hear footsteps as the guests leave. After a short while the motorbikes are gunned into action and they roar off down the road, leaving you alone with Master.

You hear Master busying himself around the house, clearing up stuff and moving furniture around.

Master releases your ankles, legs and neck from the table then loosens the chain pulling your head back. Slowly and carefully he gets you off the table and stands you on the floor. You are unsteady to start with but Mater holds you tightly until you stop swaying. He releases the O-ring and you sigh with relief at having some control over your mouth and jaws. With your tongue you feel the stomach tube. Master gives you two glasses of a protein drink mixed with milk. You are hungry and gulp it down.

'You did well tonight boy. The weekend is just beginning and by the end of it you can be sure you will be well known in the district'.

After you finish drinking Master inserts a pecker gag, which, although not as large as the pump-up gag, fills your mouth comfortably. He straps this firmly at the back of your neck. Then he pushes you forward onto the table and kicks your legs apart so that your arse, once again, is wide open. More lubricant is massaged into your hole followed by a large butt plug, which slips in easily because of the all the stretching your arse has had this evening. Master attaches the plug to small chains which encircle your balls and cock at the front and go up your arse crack at the back, to be fixed to a steel belt, which Master locks around your waist. He tightens the chains so that there is no chance to push the butt plug out. Master then gently lays you on the floor on your front. You feel a pole being pushed down your back, between your bound arms and your back, to lay the full length of your body. Master proceeds to tie you to the pole by a series of straps around your ankles, knees, thighs, stomach, chest, neck and around your forehead. These are pulled tight so that there is no movement possible between you and the pole. Master adjusts the catheter and stomach tube and ensures your nose tubes are still free. You then feel Master lift up the head end of the pole so that it rests on some object, presumably a chair. Then the foot end is lifted to the same height so that you are suspended about a metre from the floor by the pole, like a pig on a spit. The straps bite into your flesh but you are powerless to do anything about it. Master walks away.

And there you stay, bound, gagged, plugged, catheterized and covered in rubber, hanging from a pole in some house in the middle of nowhere. The only thing that keeps you sane is the belief that Master is experienced and seems gentle and kind. You do not think he will allow anything dangerous to happen to you, but you have been proved wrong in the past. Your breathing comes easily through the nose tubes and urine continues to pass silently from your bladder to your stomach. Spit dribbles out from around the gag. There is nothing in your bowels, so you don't have to worry about wanting to take a shit. The butt plug feels comfortable and reminds you of all the abuse you have had up there this evening. The metal ball ring pulls your balls down but this is not painful. You do not realize it at the time but Master has rigged up an intercom and video system, so that he can both see and hear you, should you run into any trouble.

You have lost all sense of time. You hang there, trying to come to terms with your bondage and servitude. You realize this is what you want, what you need. You feel you were born to be a slave to other men, to satisfy their sexual urges, to serve their every need and depravity. You relish your situation and look forward to what else Master Peter might have in store for you.

Mercifully the night is not warm. You are sweating inside your rubber suit but as you settle down, you do not feel hot. You drift off to sleep, waking every now and then with a start and momentary panic as you wonder why you can't move or talk. The breathing tubes whistle as your breathing gives away your temporary panic. The night seems long. You have no idea when the sun rises but eventually you hear sounds in the house and suspect that Master Peter is getting up. The sound of water running confirms this. You are relieved that the night is over.

Your hands and arms are numb. They have been tied tightly behind your back for 12 hours. Your arse is without tone as it has been plugged or fucked for 18 hours. You jaws ache from one gag or another and your nose, with its tubes, starts to feel sore. You no longer feel your balls as the heavy metal ring has been stretching them all night. Even the catheter through your cock to your bladder is starting to irritate.

You feel Master lower the pole and undo the straps. Slowly some feeling comes back to your limbs. He removes all your chains and rope bindings and stands you up. He takes out the butt plug and gently wipes your arse, but there is no mess. He removes the gag and you swallow the stale spit that has collected around it. Master commands you to kneel and you do so, without question.

'You've been a good slave so far. I am very happy with you. Today you will earn your keep on the farm and tonight we are going out. For most of the day you will be chained and wear the ball ring. The bladder catheter will remain also. Whenever you see or hear me coming you are to look to the ground. If I catch you looking at me or any other person, you will be discharged. Is that clear?'

'Yes Sir,' you reply without hesitation.

With that he removes your rubber bondage suit, the stomach tube and the nose tubes. He clamps the catheter. Your eyes slowly adjust to the faint light in the house. You down cast your eyes and focus on the floor, which is of roughly hewn planks. Some stains on the floor attest to previous activities in the house and some fresh damp patches are caused by your dribble and sweat.

Master walks away and you hear the sound of water running.

'Get in the shower and clean yourself up,' commands Master.

You thankfully walk to the next room and wash in the warm water. You notice that almost every room is kitted out as some form of dungeon. Crosses, chairs, chains, straps, hoods and whips are everywhere. In one corner a hangman's noose hangs from a scaffold and you shudder at the sight. You also notice expensive camera and video equipment and you suspect that last night's activities have been recorded. You wash away the dried sweat and try to get the lubricant out of your nose and arse. Your balls hang low because of the metal ring but you are able to wash around your cock and balls.

You quickly dry yourself and, without asking, kneel on the bathroom floor with your hands behind your back and eyes cast down. All you see is Master's high leg boots as he walks towards you.

'Good slave boy. It seems you are learning fast; I like that. Nothing worse than a boy you have to slap around the head every minute because he can't follow orders. Now get into the bedroom and dress in the clothes on the bed. Assume the position when your have dressed.'

With balls and catheter swaying you walk slowly to the bedroom. The first thing you notice on the leather-covered bed is a pair of leather shorts, with holes at the front and back. These fit snugly and you pull your catheterized cock and balls with metal ring through the front hole. A wide heavy leather collar has D rings attached front and back and at both sides. You fit this around your neck, being sure to do it up as tightly as possible. Wrist and ankle leather bracelets have locking buckles and you secure these. There is no key obvious to unlock these bracelets. The only other item is a pair a tall boots which you put on over a pair of thin black socks. You glance at a mirror and notice how hot you look. At the same time you believe you will not be allowed to enjoy this freedom for much longer.

You assume the position, on your knees, hands behind your back and head bowed.

A bowl of cereal and milk with a spoon, some bread and a mug of coffee is placed in front of you.

'Eat,' Master commands.

Without raising your head, you slowly eat the food. You're very hungry but you are aware that you have not eaten much in the past four days and don't want to bring it all back, so you relish each slowly chewed mouthful. The coffee washes it all down and, for the first time in two days, you feel reasonably human.

Master clears away the plates and puts a toothbrush and mug of water in front on you. You could weep with gratitude for the opportunity to clean your teeth. After the gags, lubricant from the stomach tube then being fucked in the mouth, it feels and tastes like a sewer. You brush vigorously and rinse with clean water, spitting into a bowl.

'To start with you can clean out the barn. Get up and walk ahead of me.'

Master pushes you out of the house, and for the first time you notice that the house is really a tumbledown shack in the middle of the forest. A barn stands to one side and Master pushes you through the front doors. Inside, bails of hay, equipment for horses and old items of farm machinery and tools lie everywhere. Shit, you think, what a mess.

'OK boy, get to and clean up this place. I don't care where you put stuff just stack it out of the way. Put the bails of hay against the wall so my friends can sit on them.'

Friends! What friends, you think. Is this going to be the place for yet another party?

'There's water in the barrel outside and you should drink plenty to flush the piss out of your system. Stand up.'

You stand and Master releases the clamp on your catheter. Urine pours onto the dirt floor of the barn and rapidly soaks away. The clamp is refastened.

'Don't touch this again until I say so, or else.' And with that, Master leaves the barn.

Nothing could be further from your mind, than to disobey this Master from heaven. You stand and survey the barn. Sunlight streams in through the open door and holes in the wooden walls. Apart from the stuff strewn about the floor, you notice chains hanging from the ceiling, coils of rope on hooks on the walls and some pieces of gym equipment in one of the horseboxes. The place looks well used and there is not much dust around, but it's just like a bomb has hit the place. You're standing there in boots, shorts with your cock, balls and arse hanging out and collared, wondering where to start. It's getting warm and you are glad to be almost naked.

You start by humping the hay toward the walls then putting all the lose tools and equipment behind the bails. You tidy the rope coils and place them on the hooks on the wall and rearrange the gym equipment so that each item is separate and accessible. Some loose D rings and padlocks you place in a dish on a shelf. You put the trash in a bin. Amongst the trash you notice old condom packets, beer cans and empty lubricant tubes. Definitely a party place, you think. You sweep the dirt floor with an old broom you find in the corner.

After two hours cleaning you're sweating and very thirsty. You go outside and drink cupfuls of water and use a wet rag to wipe the sweat from your body. The sun is high and you go inside to rest in the shade. Sitting on a bail of hay, you soon drift into sleep, to be rudely awakened by a kick in the ribs by Master's booted foot.

'What the fuck do you think you are doing boy? Did I say you could go to sleep? Get over there,' and with that, he roughly pushes you towards the centre of the barn.

You remember to look at the floor but you see Master's booted legs and leather chaps with his enormous cock swinging freely. He grabs your wrists and padlocks them together. In one swift move he pulls a hood over your head and tightens it under your chin. The hood has no eyeholes but the mouth hole is open. Two small holes over your nostrils allow you to breathe. Without warning he stuffs a sock in your mouth and ties it in place with a strap around your head. Next you hear chains clanking as your wrists are attached to chains hanging from the roof rafters. You hear a ratchet noise as Master pulls on the free end of the chain and raises your wrists. Soon you are standing on your toes. You feel your ankles pulled apart as Master ties them to the barn wall. Your balls and catheter hang down between your widely separated legs. The pain in your wrists becomes a dull ache, and there you stand, spread-eagled, hooded, collared and gagged.

'You can stay there for an hour. When I say work I mean work, not sleep.' And with that you hear Master leave the barn again.

No amount of squirming around relieves the discomfort. Your legs feel as though they are about to split apart and your arms start to ache. After a while you desperately want to piss but the catheter is clamped and all you can do is hang there.

You must have dozed off because you wake with a start as a whip cuts into your back. You gasp into your gag as more lashes cut your back and thighs. Each lash sends you juddering in your shackles, increasing the pain in your arms and legs. Master counts up to twenty, each lash being more severe than the one before. Sweat pours form your body and drips onto the dirt floor.

After twenty lashes you hang limply in your chains. You hear Master breathing heavily and realize that the effort has exhausted him also. You start again as he throws cold water over you. As you hang there, dripping, Master undoes the catheter and you groan with relief as piss pours onto the floor. As the final drops of piss fall and as you start to dry off from your drenching, Master releases your legs and slowly lowers your arms. You are unable to support yourself and crumple in a heap on the dirt floor. Master releases your wrist chains but padlocks the cuffs behind your back and leaves you there on the urine and water soaked dirt.

After an hour or so you find the strength to stand up but, realizing there is nowhere to run to, especially naked and cuffed, you sit on one of the hay bails. After a further 30 minutes, by which time you are wondering what other possible ways Master can abuse you, he returns with a sack full of gear. First he makes you drink two large glasses of the protein drink, which taste good, and you soon feel your strength return.

'Don't cross me again boy or you'll be discharged. Consider the flogging this morning as a small token of what could happen if you annoy me or any of my guests. I demand absolute obedience, is that clear?'

'Yes Sir, sorry Sir,' you say as clearly as you can, but Master kicks you in the balls anyway.

'What's that boy?'

'Sir, yes Sir,' you shout, being careful to keep your eyes fixed on his boots.

'OK, stand up.'

You shakily get to your feet. Still cuffed, Master pushes you outside and sits you beneath a tap on the wall of the barn. The cold water makes you suck in your breath but you are grateful to be able to wash away some of the crud that is covering you. Master roughly washes you down with soap and a brush, leaving you in the sun to dry. You sigh with relieve. The sun feels so good on your skin and you turn round so that every part is warmed and dried in its rays.

'Get back here boy,' Master commands from inside the barn. You amble slowly back and, anxious to please Master, assume the position without prompting. You notice that Master has spread some gear out on the dirt floor and has put the gym horse out into the main part of the barn. What alarms you is the sight of a large butt plug fixed to the centre of the horse.

PART 3

It seems there is no end to the torture. You've been covered in rubber, bound, gagged, plugged, catheterized, forced to drink your own piss, fucked in the mouth and up the arse, strung up and flogged, to say nothing of spending the night suspended in rubber from a pole. Master certainly has a wild imagination but you wonder how much more you can take. As you kneel there on the dirt floor, hands cuffed behind your back, catheter and balls hanging down you feel confident that should you reach your limit, Master would stop. He has displayed uncommon gentleness and skill to ensure that you reach the end of any endurance he imposes. He obviously knows how to take a slave to the limit and stretch him beyond it.

'We are having some more guests around soon and you will be the centre of attention again. It's a slave auction and whoever bids highest will have the use of you for an hour. You will not leave the property and I will keep a distant eye on things to make sure they do not get out of hand.'

You've always fantasized about being sold at an auction, but worried if some crazy bought you and you were never heard of again. This arrangement of Masters seems organised and controlled. What more could they do that has not been done already?

'OK boy, stand up and bend forwards.'

You obey instantly. Master takes a tub of lubricant and generously slathers it into your arse, then onto the butt plug on the horse. He roughly pushes you up onto the horse, with a hay bail either side for your feet, then he forces you down onto the butt plug. It seems larger than the multi-lobed one last night, but your arse expands to accommodate it all. The last few inches are swallowed by your arse with difficulty, but Master pushes you down onto it as you groan with pain. At the end the plug narrows considerably and your arse tightens around the neck of the plug. You feel the enormous mass of it in your arse.

Master pulls the hay bails away and ties your ankles beneath the horse. There is no way you can relieve the pressure in your arse, you are just stuck there by the plug. He attaches a small chain to the ball ring and pulls it painfully forward so that your erect cock stands out in front of you, with the catheter pointing upwards. He attaches the chain to a fixture on the horse, making sure it is taught. Master stands on a bail and quickly pulls the rubber hood over your head, tightening the neck collar and fastening it with a padlock. The mouth hole is quickly filled with a tube gag, into which Master tapes a tube attached to the end of the catheter. You feel the end of the tube in your mouth and soon taste your own piss as Master removes the clamp. You have no alternative but to swallow your piss. You soon get used to the slightly bitter taste of warm piss. You feel your wrists being drawn backwards and upwards, which forces your head forwards and down, as Master attaches a chain to your cuffed wrists and lifts them to a beam on the roof. A last chain is attached to the back of you collar and the other end of the chain to the beam, pulling your head backwards again.

You think you must have looked a pretty sight, fixed to the horse by the butt plug, hooded and gagged with your arms and neck painfully pulled backwards. The slightest twitch pulls on your balls, wrenches your arms or neck or sends shudders of pain up your arse.

The only sound reaching your ears was the sound of Master's boots on the dirt floor as he leaves the barn.

As time passes your attention wanders from one pain to another. Periodically you squirm to relieve the pressure in your arse, but that sends spasms of pain through your stretched balls, so you just sit quietly and imagine what will happen next.

You estimate you have been fixed on the butt plug for two hours. It's hot as hell in the barn and sweat runs down your body and from between your legs. Your piss tastes stronger than usual and you suspect you are getting dehydrated. Still, in your dark world of pain, you would not be anywhere else.

Cars draw up outside and you detect the thud of booted feet entering the barn. The smell of leather reaches you as men circle you, pulling on your tits and tweaking your erect cock. There is much complementary chatter about how good the slave looks. Master explains the rules of the auction. The highest bidder will have use of you for one hour, the next highest bidder for 45 mins and so on. However, men can add their times together and both use you for the total time. There will be no unsafe sex and Master will observe from a distance, to make sure that play is not too extreme. What could possibly be more extreme than what you have been subjected to already?

The beer flows freely and after an hour the bidding starts. Quickly one Master takes control of the bidding and bids the others out of contention. You hear Master Peter summarize the times for your abuse and in your mind you add it all up to 3 hours. With that Master Peter unties your feet and releases the chains around your balls, neck and hands and places two bails beneath your feet so that you can push yourself off the butt plug. You force yourself to take the searing pain in your arse as the widest part of the plug comes out, followed by the remainder, which just slides out. You stand there, gagged, hooded and collared with your hands cuffed behind you.

You detect strange hands around you. A leash is attached to your collar and you are pulled out of the barn and into the forest. It's cooler out in the forest but you wonder whom you are with and what he will do to you. First the gag is removed and replaced by an O-ring gag. A chain forces your wrists up to the back of your neck so that your head is once again pulled backwards. The clicking of padlocks means this is a semi permanent arrangement. Gently you are lowered on your front to the ground. You feel chains being attached to your ankles and your legs are pulled wide apart and attached to nearby trees.

Although you are immobilized and painfully tied and chained, you are happy to be on the ground, which is cool. After a short while you hear footsteps around you and some chatter; obviously the Master has been joined by others. Little do you know you are to be used as the public toilet for the next few hours. You hear zips open then a rush of warm urine soaks you on the back and legs. You feel degraded and dirty, being used as another man's piss pig. No amount of struggling can get you out of the way of the piss and the more your squirm, the more you just stir up a mud bath.

Without notice your head is grasped firmly at the sides and your open mouth is impaled on a thick cock. The Master sits down in front of your head with his legs at your sides and proceeds to fuck you in the mouth. When his hands are removed your head naturally falls onto the cock, so there is no way to avoid having in at the back of your throat. You taste the latex condom, with relief. Then, without notice, you feel another cock enter your arse and start fucking the living daylights out of you. Both Masters are not gentle so you know that Master Peter is not amongst them. You are used to this being fucked at both ends at the same time but the ferocity of these new Masters takes your breath away. On and on they thrust. At full thrust by the cock up your arse, you are forced further onto the cock in your mouth and you gag when the cock hits the back of your throat.

Eventually both Masters shoot their loads then leave you in the piss soaked mud, gasping and periodically squirting air and lube out your arse. These are the rape scenes you had always fantasized about, and with Master Peter in the background, you are happy that everything is under control.

Just as you start to doze off, some one releases your legs and stands you up. This Master seems gentle as he releases the padlocked chain which is forcing your arms up and head back. Miraculously he then takes off the hood and gag so that you can see again. Your hands are still cuffed behind you and the ankle cuffs are still on, but the relief is tremendous. You are so grateful, albeit a little unsteady. Firm hands grasp you around the waste as you sway unsteadily. Slowly your eyes adjust to the evening light and to the handsome, bearded face in front of you. This new Master is wearing boots outside his chaps and a cock ring. He has two nipple rings but his chest is bare. He firmly grasps your head and locks his mouth to yours in an affectionate, tongue-probing kiss. He forces you to drink some water, then a can of beer, which is heavenly. He says his name is Mark, Master Mark.

You wonder how this Master can be so different to the other two but your thoughts are cut short when he produces a leather collar and leash. When the collar is firmly locked in place, he attaches the leash and pulls you another 50 metres into the forest. Clearly he has plans, other than affectionate kissing, for you.

You notice a clearing between four short trees, where he has left rope and a jumble of gags and collars. He leads you to the middle of the clearing and quietly releases the leash and removes the padlock from your wrists. You take a look at your hands for the first time in over a day. He releases the clamp on the catheter to allow piss to flow freely onto the ground, then clamps it again. As you stand there in the fading light you notice how strong and handsome this Master is. You wonder if you will see him again after this weekend.

Gently Master Mark tells you to lie on your back on the grass, which you do immediately. Not so gently he ties you spread eagled to the four trees, by ropes through the wrist and ankle cuffs. He strains hard to stretch you to the limit before tying off the ropes at each corner. You feel the cuffs biting into your wrists and ankles, and the pull on you arms as they strain in their shoulder sockets.

Master Mark positions himself over your chest and kneels so that his enormous condom covered cock is directly in front of your face. He grabs your head and forces his cock into your mouth, which opens to accept it keenly. He pumps it in and out, but never deeply or roughly. You glance up at his face, to notice he has his eyes closed and an expression of tranquillity on his face. As his cock gets harder your jaw is stretched to the limit. You are careful to keep your teeth out of the way because you don't want to bite him or break the condom. After endless thrusting he blows a huge stream of cum into the condom, and only at this time, pushes his cock into the far reaches of your throat, so that you gag and struggle for breath.

No sooner has he blown his load than he swings round and tells you to clean his arse. As your eager tongue probes his sweet arse he strokes your cock, which immediately comes to attention. He then bends forward to take your cock into his warm and welcoming mouth; at the same time he thrusts his cock into yours. You are in seventh heaven, doing 69's with this handsome

Master. Up and down, up and down he goes, but never so much as to enable you to start that short journey to ejaculation.

You hear a bell ring, which is the signal for drinks, and Master Mark gets up without speaking. He rips off the used condom and stuffs it in a trash bag. As he leaves you spread-eagled on the ground you wonder who will come next. All you hear are his footsteps disappearing into the forest.

PART 4

The light fades to darkness. Is nobody going to release you from this position? By this time your arms are aching and your bladder needs emptying. You realize you are at least 100 metres from the house, and crying out for help brings no response. You wonder what kind of animals are lurking around in the forest; Master Peter mentioned wolves. You try struggling against the ropes but Master Mark made no mistake when he fixed you in that spread-eagled position.

A damp mist envelopes the forest and you start to shiver. As the moon rises a light rain falls to chill you even further. You realize you have not been cold so far this weekend, having been encased in rubber, then forced to work. You shiver violently.

As the rain eases you hear footsteps approaching. Master Peter looms from the shadows. You suspect he has not been far away. Without speaking he releases you and removes the leather cuffs from your wrists and ankles. He opens the catheter and you sigh as piss pours onto the ground. Your relief is, however, short lived. Master produces the rubber, eyeless hood, which he locks around your neck, and then inserts a ball gag, which he fastens at the back of your neck. Handcuffs secure your wrists behind you. He inserts a butt plug, which he fixes in place with chains connected to the metal waistband. The leash is attached to the collar and he pulls you forwards. You stumble at first but he guides you across open ground and steadies you when you trip.

The sound of partying alerts you that you are nearing the house. Inside the house you smell beer, but Master takes you straight through the main room to the back room. He leaves you standing while he disappears into the main room. You catch snippets of conversation. Words like lynch, hang, display, flog, make you shudder. After a short time someone grabs and forces you onto your knees. The hood is removed but the gag remains. You notice it is the first Master who seems to have repossessed you. He backs you up to beneath the hangman's noose, placing it firmly around your neck and cinches it tight. The rope passes over a beam and he pulls the free end down and ties it off on the wall. Without ceremony he uses rope to tie your feet and knees together, then proceeds to tie your arms to your chest. You relieve the pressure on your noosed neck by standing on tiptoe, but eventually your feet tire and you take the pressure again around your neck. As a final gesture he applies cruel tit clamps connected by a heavy chain, but all you can do is groan, and tears flow down your cheeks.

'It's done,' he announces to the main room.

The two other Masters and Master Peter enter and sit on chairs around the room. You can hardly believe what is happening. Surely they do not intend to hang you.

The first Master, who seems to know all about hanging, announces that anyone can be hung for a few seconds and then revived. Your eyes plea with Master Peter to stop this craziness, but he seems comfortable and relaxed.

Amyl is produced and held to your nose. As your head starts to swim you feel the rope tighten, and tighten. You feel yourself loosing consciousness and the last thing you remember is your feet leaving the ground as you jerk upwards. The next thing you know, you are lying on the ground with the noose loosened and the gag out, but you are still bound and cuffed. You notice the Masters are masturbating over you, but they are careful not to shoot their loads.

'Yeah boy, did you enjoy being hung up?' The first Master asks.

Before you can answer the noose is used to pull you back to your feet, then tightened. Someone removes the ropes fixing the butt plug and pulls it out. You are barely able to stand and would certainly fall over were it not for the noose. Your relief from the butt plug is short lived as someone thrusts himself into your arse. You realize it is Master Peter, since everyone else is standing around in front of you. Slowly he fucks you, and it would have been good were it not for the noose around your neck. He stands on a low stool and this enables him to get better penetration of your arse. Without warning, more amyl is produced and you start to sink again. Before the amyl has maximum effect you feel the noose tighten again and slowly your feet leave the ground again. You remain conscious while Master fucks you furiously but loose consciousness shortly after.

You have no idea how long you are out. You wake up to silence in the room, lying bound and gagged on the floor. The noose is gone. A neck collar is anchoring you to the floor via a padlock, and your bound feet are fixed to the far wall with rope. You are on your front so all you see is the stained wooden floor. Mercifully your arse is empty, although judging by the amount of wind you are passing you suspect you have been fucked by several men whilst unconscious. Your nipples are killing you and you remember the heavy clamps and wonder if they are still on.

The night drags on. Where the fuck is everyone, you ask yourself? The occasional bump startles you, but you cannot move. You suspect the catheter is open because you feel no pressure in your bladder. As it turns out, piss is draining into a bag tied to your leg. How much longer can you take this, you wonder? You ache all over and you get no relief by trying to move. All that does is put strain on your neck. It's as much as you can do to put your head sideways to rest. Your cuffed hands are numb and your balls ache from the heavy ring locked around them.

As the day breaks you detect movement in the room. You cannot see anything but you suspect that someone is watching you. After what seems an eternity Master Peter looms into view, his powerful frame silhouetted against the window. Remembering the rules, you dare not look directly at him.

'You OK boy?'

All you can do is grunt once, meaning yes.

'It's Sunday and the weekend is nearly over. I'm going to release you now but I have a proposition to make.'

Gently he releases your neck collar and gag and unties your arms and legs. He takes the cuffs off and massages some life into your numb hands. Slowly he gets you to your feet and guides you to one of the chairs. You notice the catheter and bag and the heavy ball ring bangs against the edge of the chair as you sit. More alarming, you notice your nipples have been pierced, with two small padlocks locked into place through the holes. There is a small amount a dried blood around the padlocks. That explains the pain in your nipples.

'You can look at me now boy,' commands Master.

You notice this strong and gentle man. He is dressed in leather pants and boots and a black shirt. His hairy chest is muscular and his biceps bulge as he lifts you. His close-cropped hair sets off his chiselled features.

'You did well boy. You've been put through the most extreme bondage, you've been fucked in the mouth and arse by seven men, you've been hung by the neck until you pass out, and all this has been recorded on video. I am an honest man and together we will make some money from the film. 50/50 OK? I know lots of people who will pay big bucks for this stuff.'

'Yes Sir,' is all you can reply.

'Well boy, what do you think? How did you find it?'

'I had a great time Sir. It's more than I ever dreamed about. Thank you Sir. It's a pity it's Sunday though.'

'Yeah, sure is a pity. But hey, remember Master Mark, he wants to see you again. I had a word with him on the quiet when the others had gone, and while he helped me fix you to the floor last night. He said he'd be interested in a semi permanent arrangement, to share you with me some weekends. How does that sound to you?'

'Great. I like Master Mark out of all the other men here. Like you, he seems experienced and gentle.'

'Yeah, he's like me; works in the city; great house in town with a cellar, which he has converted into a dungeon. He's big on making films too and he likes taking his slaves to showings at the BDSM club in town. How does that sound?'

'Terrific Sir. It's my fantasy to be bound and displayed like last night.'

'Then it's done boy. One thing though. Whilst you will be free to go home today, that heavy ball ring remains. While you were out to it last night we welded the thing, so that it cannot be removed. It will be a permanent reminder of whom you belong to. It's loose enough to let the blood flow, but you will not be able to get it off. Of course, we keep the keys to the padlocks through your nipples and they will not be removed for a long time. Also, every night when you get home from work, you are to put that butt plug in and leave it there all night. We've no way to know if you will do this, but we think you will because you want to come back to see us. We will know when we fuck you if you have not used the butt plug.'

'Sir, I will do it. And the catheter, Sir?'

Master produces a syringe, empties the retaining balloon and pulls the catheter out. You briefly jump as it plops out but settle back into the chair, relieved to be rid of the thing.

'That may go back in from time to time, OK?'

'Yes Sir.'

'Every moment of every day you remember you are a slave. Whenever you take a piss, you will feel the heavy ball ring; whenever you shower you will see the nipple padlocks; whenever you go to bed, you will feel the butt plug. You will be a permanent slave, OK?'

'I am happy with this Sir. I know I was born to be a slave, to be abused by strong men and kept in chains and shackles. Whenever I can, I will serve you both. You will not be disappointed Sir?'

"I know boy. As time passes you will help us induct other slaves and you may even be allowed to fuck one or two of them. This is a growing thing boy and we need as many slaves as possible to service Masters.'

'I understand Sir.'

On the train back home that afternoon you reflect on the weekend's experiences. When you started this journey, in trepidation, you were not to know that it would be the most rewarding experience of your life. You had dreamed for ages of being kept bound and gagged, plugged and hooded, without control of your body, for the amusement of Masters, to be abused, fucked, raped, whipped, forced to work, displayed and humiliated and degraded for the pleasure of others. Your dream has been fulfilled but more, you have entered a new state of consciousness. Whilst you go about your daily business, earning wages, having a drink with friends and chatting with relatives you will always realize that you don't really have any control over your life. The ball ring, nipple padlocks and, at night, the butt plug, will remind you that your body will always belong to others.

PART 5

After an hour of sitting in the train your padlocked nipples start to ache. You presume Master Peter had used local anaesthetic when piercing your nipples and inserting the small padlocks. Now, two hours later, every jolt of the train sends knives of pain through your nipples. You think this will last a couple of days and wonder how you will deal with work in your office. Fortunately you sit at a desk most of the day and there should not be a problem, but you will have to forget about squash and gym workouts for a week. Standing up in the train, there is less pain from your nipples, but the welded metal ball ring pulls your balls into the base of the ball sack and this is another pain to be reckoned with.

Despite your pain you are very happy. You have endured a weekend of unforgettable bondage, torture and rape but you have enjoyed every minute of it. You felt safe in the hands of Master Peter, and on the second day you had met Master Mark, who had promised to be in touch with you. Despite the fact that Master Peter had invited his friends to tie and abuse you, he made sure you came to no harm.

You are calm and at peace with yourself. All your petty worries and work problems seem ridiculously trivial and you vouch to forget about them.

Everything seems so much clearer now. This enables you to focus on the bigger picture of your life, your work and your future. The first decision you make will be to go work for the accounting firm in the city, which had promised you a senior position. You were noncommittal when they offered you the job last week, thinking it would be disloyal of you to leave your current firm. You now realize there are larger things in life than loyalty to some small accounting firm in the suburbs. You will resign first thing tomorrow and take up the city offer. The second decision you make will be to be positive about your future. There is no reason why you should not try those new management strategies at the new firm, as they were sure to make you and the firm a fortune. Yes, things will change from now on.

As the train nears the city your mind wanders to Master Mark. Master Peter did not mind when he said he wanted to meet you later. In fact Master Peter seemed almost pleased with this arrangement. You know they are good friends and both successful businessmen in the city. Like Master Peter, Master Mark seems gentle, compared to the rough handling from the other Masters over the weekend. He was firm, knew what he wanted, but in forcing you to comply, he was gentle and affectionate. You knew you would be safe in his hands.

Both Masters have given strict instructions, that the butt plug must be inserted every night and tied in place. You know you will do this unfailingly. The ball ring and nipple padlocks will remain in place until they decide otherwise. You are bound to them as much by the physical evidence as by their trust in you as a slave.

It is dark by the time you get home so you shower and prepare for bed. As you insert the butt plug you immediately get an erection, then realize that despite being erect for the whole weekend, you had not actually shot your load. You beat off furiously and a massive amount of cum splashes over the bathroom floor. As you view your naked body in front of the mirror, with its padlocks and ball ring and the ropes tying in the butt plug, you get erect again. You suspect this will be an ongoing problem and the only way you can avoid beating off repeatedly is to cuff your hands. You lie on your bed and cuff your hands behind your back. Immediately you feel the memories of the weekend surging back and feel calm. You sleep soundly.

The alarm screams and you wake up with a start. You try to turn it off and only succeeded in banging your head on the table and nearly tearing your nipples off. It takes you ages to get the key in the cuffs, release yourself and get ready for work. In order to hide the impression of the nipple padlocks on your white business shirt, you wear an undershirt. Fortunately the ball ring is hidden in your pants, but you still feel the pressure on your balls when you stand up.

At work you confirm that the new position is still open and the manager said he looked forward to having you start next week. Your boss is not happy that you are leaving but suggests there are more accountants where you came from, reconfirming your resolve to get out at the end of the week, at the same time you wonder why you had stuck it so long. Loyalty was not even skin deep with this crowd.

In the afternoon you get two phone calls. The first is from your new manager, who said to be sure to bring your social security card next week. Before he hangs up he says how much he enjoyed meeting you at the weekend. Before you can answer, he is gone. What did he mean, meeting you at the weekend? You have never seen him before. Was he one of the Masters at Master Peter's house? That's the only possible way he could have met you. You thought the circle of BDSM Masters in town was small; now it seems to be bursting out in all directions.

The other phone call is from Master Mark. He immediately has your full attention and, as he speaks, you find yourself answering him with '…. Sir.' How easily you had become a slave. Master Mark says he has put in a good word for you at your new firm and that you will have no trouble settling in. You wondered last week how you had been offered the job by just sending your resume; not even an interview. Now you realize that Master Mark is a significant person in the city and when he says something, people jump. You relish the thought of serving this powerful man. He tells you that he is arranging something for the weekend, so not to make any other arrangements.

Arrangements! You have forgotten all about your other friends and are prepared to let everything go, except serving your Masters. From then on, whenever you feel the tug of the ball ring or when the nipple padlocks catch on your shirt, you surge with enthusiasm, not only for the prospects of the weekend, but also for your work. Your colleagues comment that you must be on drugs, you seem so happy and keen. They are even more surprised when they hear that you have resigned, expecting you to loose all interest in your current job. Not so. Life was there to enjoy and you put your everything into every moment of it.

On the Thursday Master Mark phones you with instructions for the weekend. You will be his entry at an exhibition of slaves at the local leather club. You had been to the club once but were shy and did not mix with the others. Now you will be exhibited for all to see and despite your shyness, will have no control over what will happen. The idea gets you hard immediately and you hope it does not show through your pants. His instructions are to start on the liquid protein diet, so that you would not be full of shit. Also be sure you get a No 1 buzz cut. Three enemas the evening beforehand; butt plug tied in place, chaps, boots, leather jacket, then just wait in your apartment. You know your head will not remain uncovered for long. Master Mark says he has a hood for you.

That evening you visit the hairdressers for a No 1 hair cut. You feel much more the slave when you see yourself in the mirror with hardly any hair left on your head.

You throw yourself back into your work and even on your last day you complete more accounts that the rest of the office put together. As you clear out your desk you can hardly contain your excitement at leaving, but you bid everyone a warm goodbye.

You rush home and immediately start the enema preparations. From the start the water is almost clear so you are happy you will not get punished for leaving shit in there. You decide to use a slightly larger butt plug, which you have just purchased. The old butt plug slips in very easily during its nightly insertion and you are afraid it will fall out, despite being firmly tied in place. The new plug slides in after a struggle and your arse clamps around the base. You wrap the rope around your waist and then between your legs and over the plug, spreading it around your cock and ball ring, and tying it front and back. Next the chaps and boots feel snug and they emphasize the ball ring and butt plug. The plug feels comfortable when you are standing, but is painful when you sit on a chair, as it is forced deeper into your arse.

Five minutes to go and you assume the position of subservience in the hallway, on your knees, hands behind your back and looking at the floor. The roar of a motorbike fades as it enters the car park under your apartment building. Two minutes later you hear the thud of booted feet on the stairs outside your door. You have left he door unlocked and within a few seconds you see a pair of knee-high boots and leather covered muscular legs standing before you. The smell of leather and exhaust fumes is powerful.

Without saying anything, Master Mark walks past you and into the living room. You dare not look and your eyes cast down to the floor. You hear the thump of a heavy bag as it drops to the floor, then the chink of glass as Master pours himself a drink from your extensive liquor collection. You rarely drink but always keep a comprehensively stocked drinks cabinet for friends.

'Here boy. Crawl over to me,' commands Master.

With head bowed you crawl on all fours to Master's booted feet. He lifts his feet up onto your back and crosses his legs, using you as a footstool. The weight of his booted feet and his muscular legs cause your back to sink and you struggle to keep it from sagging. Master flicks on the TV to watch the evening stock market reports, congratulating himself as the report indicates that he has made another small fortune today.

When Master Mark finishes his drink he takes his feet off you and sinks into the chair.

'Turn around and look at me boy,' he says in a commanding way that leaves no room for discussion.

You swivel around to look him in the face. At first his appearance takes your breath away. You remembered his handsome features from the previous weekend. His chiselled features and muscular frame attest to many hours spent in the gym. He is well groomed and wears expensive leather clothes. A gold watch glints from beneath the cuff of his leather jacket. When he speaks it is with a cultured accent, confirming a privileged upbringing.

'OK boy, this is the scene. This weekend you are mine. Understand?'

'Yes Sir,' you reply without hesitation.

'Tonight is the Annual Exhibition of Slaves at the leather club. You will be my exhibit. You will be taken to the club as a slave and for the entire evening you will be kept bound. At the club, slaves will be put into three positions and slaves will be judged on these positions and anything else the Master does with the slave. For the moment you don't need to know any more details. Masters and slaves will arrive early so that slaves can be prepared before the others arrive.'

'I understand Sir.' You are thrilled with this prospect of public bondage and servitude, but wonder what the 'anything else' refers to. Whipping maybe. Fucking, probably not, but Master is very liberated and it might be part of the act he had in mind. Whatever, you are sure you will not have any say in the activities.

'If at any time you complain, or decide you don't want to continue, you can nod your head three times and you will be released. At that point you will discontinue any relationship with me. Understand?'

'Yes Sir. That will not happen Sir.'

'Good, now face away and put your hands behind you.'

Handcuffs are deftly applied and locked to prevent tightening. The cuffs are much heavier than your own and you suspect they are genuine prison cuffs. Next Master pulls a leather hood over your head. The hood has pinholes for the eyes and a hole for the mouth. He cinches it by tightly, tying the cords at the back and threads a studded collar through the holes in the neck part. The collar is fastened with a heavy padlock. Into your mouth he forces a ball gag, tightening the straps around the back of your head.

Your field of vision is limited by the pinholes but you can see immediately in front. Master then pulls a black helmet from his bag and places it over your head, fastening the chinstraps. It is impossible for anyone to see the hooded and gagged head inside. The only part that is visible is the studded collar and padlock at the back of your neck.

'OK boy, lets go.'

Master pushes you out of the door and you take the fire stairs to the car park in the basement. This way Master avoids any traffic on the main apartment stairs. You step carefully, feeling the edges of the stairs with your feet before going down. You do not want to trip and fall headfirst.

In the basement car park you can see Master's powerful bike parked in the shadows. He pushes you towards it and commands you to sit of the pillion seat. As you straddle the bike you start to loose your balance, but Master's arms are there immediately to steady you and guide you to the seat. As you lower yourself you feel the butt plug forced further into your arse and you grunt at the pain. Master places your boots on the footrests and you feel metal clamps drawn around your ankles, fixing them to the bike. With your cuffed hands you can feel the grab rail at the back of the bike, and using a padlock, Master fixes the cuffs to the rail. You grasp the rail to steady yourself, for what you know will be a 10 Km twisting journey.

Master mounts the bike and guns it into action. Within seconds you are speeding along the dark streets of the city. You grab the rail hard as the bike twists in and out of traffic and wonder how you will explain your situation to the Police if they stop the bike. At traffic lights you notice that adjacent car drivers see your cuffed hands and clamped feet and their jaws drop, but the bike speeds away before they can do anything. Occasionally a car pips its horn and you know that you have been noticed. You enjoy this anonymous enslavement, wondering if any of your colleagues of friends are seeing the spectacle, without realizing who is inside that leathered and hooded outfit.

The traffic thins as you approach the club. The entrance is down a quiet back street and you note that not many bikes or cars are parked in the parking lot. You notice a Master leading a slave by a collar and leash towards the entrance. The slave is wearing leather shorts and boots only and is cuffed and gagged. He glances at your body bound to the back of the bike as you pass.

Your mind is racing, trying to think what is in store for you tonight. You have dreamed of public bondage and humiliation and only your shyness has prevented this in the past. Now you have surrendered yourself to Master Mark and have already lost control over your fate.

The bike pulls into a parking space and dies when Master removes the key. Master removes your helmet then says 'wait here' and goes into the club, leaving you bound to the bike. Other club goers pass the bike and a few stop to look at the spectacle of a boy, in leather and boots, hooded and gagged and chained to a motorbike. You are totally unable to talk with them, or move, and their comments and laughter heighten your arousal; you know you are at their mercy if they decide to do anything to you.

Time passes. Your arse aches from the butt plug and you are beginning to wonder if Master Mark will leave you there all night.

PART 6

It seems hours before Master Mark returns. The street is filling with people going to the club. Almost everyone is in leather and boots and some are being led by collars and leashes, some wearing only shorts or leather thongs and are handcuffed, others wear harnesses and muzzles. This is obviously going to be some event. Master releases the padlock holding your cuffed wrists to the grab rail and the shackles around you ankles. He steadies you as you slide off the bike and immediately pushes you to your knees. A small crowd gathers to watch him attach a chain to your collar then yank you to your feet and pull you towards the club entrance.

As you enter you notice that slaves are already in position in the hallway. Several are naked, and tied with rope to the columns that line the sidewalls. Each one has his wrists cuffed back behind the wide columns. Their legs are manacled by a chain passing behind the column. Some have weights attached to their balls by parachutes; others have chastity devices locked in place. All are gagged with a mixture of bit gags, ball gags or duck tape and all have some form of eye cover. Each slave has either weights attached to nipple rings or nipple clamps with connecting chain and weights. They all squirm with pain as they try to relieve the pressure in their wrists, balls or nipples.

Master Mark pulls you through to the main room. In the centre is a spot lit stage and your eyes are drawn to the six metal frames that have been erected in the centre. Each frame is about three metres square with cross pieces, and fixed above by chains disappearing to the ceiling and to the floor by padlocks. You notice several Masters and slaves already on the stage.

Carefully you make your way to the steps leading to the stage, avoiding slaves on the floor licking their Master's boots or sitting, cuffed, at their Master's feet. On the stage you are placed before a frame and only then are you able to look out onto the audience. Hundreds of eyes fix on you through the glare of the spotlights. Eyes are fixed onto your exposed balls with their heavy ball ring and to the rope keeping the butt plug in place. You are blushing inside your hood and immediately start to get an erection.

The first thing Master Mark does is to uncuff you and you rub your wrists; the cuffs had bitten into your wrists from the bike journey. Next, Master Mark removes your leather jacket and the cool air is a welcome relief as you had started to sweat inside it. Master gently but firmly stands you in front of the frame and attaches leather cuffs to your wrists. To these he attaches chains, which he threads through pulleys at the corners of the frames. He pulls at the chains, lifting your arms towards the corners of the frame so that they are in line with the cross beam of the frame. Master brings the chains together over your head, threads both though another pulley at the top of the frame then brings them down and padlocks them to the back of your collar. Immediately you feel the pressure in the collar and shuffle to relieve the tension.

You are already feeling exposed and vulnerable, being strung up in front of a crowd, on a stage and in a spotlight. Your erection is starting to get painful and this adds to your excitement.

Next, Master threads chains through your ankle cuffs and pulls your feet to the bottom corners of the frame. This adds more pressure on your neck and forces you to stand on your toes, as much as your boots will allow. You are barely able to breathe as Master padlocks the ankle chains in place.

And there you are, hooded and gagged, bare-chested with your padlocked nipples exposed, your cock and balls swinging under the weight of the ball ring, butt plugged and spread-eagled in front of a crowd. It seems as though everyone is looking at you and you relish in the attention, the exposure, the humiliation. The scene defines you as some else's slave and property.

With a handful of small straps Master proceeds to tie your arms to the cross beams of the frame; one around your wrists, one at the elbows and one at the shoulders. He then places a belt around your upper chest and another around your upper abdomen and threads them through the back of the frame. This effectively anchors you to the frame and relieves some of the pressure on your wrists and neck. Next Master does the same with your legs, tying straps around your thighs, knees and ankles so that you are stretched and fixed to the cross beam in a spread eagled position, with your cock and balls swinging freely. You feel like a public slut, with every part open to public inspection. Whilst you cannot recognize any familiar faces in the audience your vision is limited by the pinholes in the mask, and you wonder if anyone would recognize you, were the hood not padlocked around your head.

Other slaves around you are being prepared. One slave is completely naked with only a bit gag in his mouth and is strung up by his wrists to the top beam. He is groaning as his Master spreads his legs to the bottom corners of the frame but the more he groans, the harder his Master pulls on the ropes. Another is bucking and squirming as his Master has him bent over and is forcing a dildo up his arse. This is then tied in place with ropes around his balls and waist. Another is handcuffed and hooded and fixed by chains from his collar to the sides of the frame and by chains around his cock and balls to the bottom beam. You cannot clearly see the others but from the periodic grunts and muffled screams you suspect that they are being strung up in some painful position.

After half an hour all the Masters leave the stage, leaving only the six slaves strung up on their frames and exposed in the spotlights. You are unable to move a muscle, your arms and legs being firmly bound to the frame and your head and neck immobilized by the chain connected to the collar. Your hooded head and gag prevent you from uttering any sound. All you can do is periodically suck in your arse to move the butt plug in and out slightly and this sets your heavy ball ring swinging, leading to pain in your balls. Your cock remains rigidly at attention and you feel precum dripping down its shaft. Never before had you been so publicly displayed. Sounds from around you suggest that some of the other slaves were not so immobilized.

The occasional groan or clank of chains indicates to you that they are writhing in their bondage.

What little you can see of the audience through the pinholes in your hood, show that they are very interested in you. After an hour some members of the audience are appointed judges and wander about the stage, making comments and scribbling notes.

After a further 10 minutes Master Mark appears and without saying anything unties the rope fixing your butt plug in place and yanks it out. You groaned deeply as the widest part of the plug passes through your arse and you are relieved when only a small amount of gas follows. Nevertheless Master wipes your arse and discards the cloth on the floor. Then, standing in front of you, so that both you and the audience can see what he is doing, he removes his own cock from his tight leather pants and with one move, encases it in a black condom. The audience anticipates what is about to happen and erupts into cheers. Carefully he strokes his cock to erection and applies a small amount of jelly before going behind you. You tremble at the thought of being publicly raped, but at the same time are excited beyond your dreams.

Slowly and with much gyrating of hips, Master Mark forces his huge cock into your arse and slowly begins pumping away. Each thrust sends your weighted balls swinging and the audience cheer. Master grasps your thighs to get better penetration so that now each thrust feels like he is drilling away at your very insides. You are immobile and without any control over your body. You are being publicly raped, and you love every minute of it. You feel Master's thrusting becoming harder and more frequent and within a few minutes he lurches forward, penetrating you with the force of a horse and you feel the warm cum filling his condom. Slowly he releases his grip on your thighs and backs up. You feel a plop as his huge cock frees itself of your arse. He deftly removes the condom before standing once again in front of you and acknowledging the cheers of the crowd. It takes forever for his erection to go down and only then, with difficulty, does he manage to force it back inside his pants.

You are sweating and breathless at the humiliation of public raping. But you are filled with immense satisfaction and pleasure. As you regulate your breathing you detect other Masters approaching their slaves. Some rape their slaves as you have been, but because of inefficient gags, the slaves groan and cry out. Some bend their slaves forward and whip them on the back and arse. Others force their slaves to kneel whilst they fuck them in the mouth. For the next hour you stand there, immobile, while this orgy of public humiliation takes place around you. Once again members of the audience in the front row are writing on clipboards and a panel is collecting marks at a side table.

Eventually all the Masters are again summoned to the stage and proceed to prepare their slaves for the third, and final act of this bizarre spectacle. Master Mark slowly unties all your bonds and has you kneel on the floor through the frame. With a wide belt he ties your back and abdomen to the underside of the crossbeam and spreads your legs to the bottom corners of the frame. Your wrists are padlocked behind your back and tied to the crossbeam. Another rope from the back of your collar is pulled upwards and tied to the crossbeam, thereby forcing your head upwards, face forward. Master removes the ball gag and offers you a drink of beer, the first drink since leaving your apartment some hours ago. Once you finish the beer he inserts a dental gag and fixes it behind your head. By slowly opening the ratchet, he spreads your jaws wide apart. Because you cannot now swallow, spittle dribbles onto the floor. Beneath you, your weighted balls swing freely and precum continues to pour from your cock.

Master then leaves the stage and waits in the audience while the other slaves are prepared. Some Masters seem not to know how to tie their slaves and make several attempts to secure them to the frame, but eventually all slaves are tied into some new position, some on their knees, others spread eagled, others upright with hands and elbows tied tightly behind their backs.

A pool of spittle has gathers beneath your head. You neck is beginning to ache and you are getting cramp in your legs. If you move, your balls start to swing, sending shock waves through them. You notice Master Mark get up from his seat and make for the stage. But he is not alone. With shock and pleasure you notice that Master Peter is joining him. You had not noticed Master Peter amidst the sea of leather and boots, but when he stood you recognized his tall, muscular features. He is bare-chested, in chaps and boots and with a military cap on. He looks devastatingly handsome.

Master Peter positions himself behind you on his knees and, without ceremony, starts to fuck you. At the same time Master Mark, having already fucked you up the arse, kneels and inserts his condom-covered cock into the depths of your mouth. The audience applauds and some move to the side of the stage to get a better view of this raping from both ends. Because Master Mark is gentle whilst fucking your mouth you do not gag. Occasionally when Master Peter is thrusting up your arse, Master Peter's cock reaches the depths of your throat and you heave. They try to synchronize their movements so that one thrusts while the pulls out. However, as the pace increases they become uncoordinated and they continue to ruthlessly pound you from both ends, sending spasms through your bound body. Eventually, both shoot their loads and lean forward to kiss each other. This brings the house down and the audience erupts into cheering.

As they leave the stage Master Mark releases your head, which slumps forwards. Your jaws remain spread wide apart but you are grateful for the release of pressure on your neck. Saliva pours from your mouth onto the floor in front of you, and you noisily pass gas from your arse, but nothing else comes out. Eventually you just hang there, wrists and body supported by the beams of the frame and arse and mouth still exposed to whomever wants to take advantage of you.

Other Masters proceed to abuse their slaves. Some whip them, causing them to shudder and jerk on the frames and scream into their gags. Others are fucked up the arse or in the mouth. The whole show lasts another hour, with continual applause and shouts of approval from the audience. Eventually the judges complete their task. Slaves, including yourself, are released from the frames and kneel in a line on the stage. Each slave is retied, and in your case Master Mark cuffs your hands behind you and reinserts the ball gag. He attaches a chain to your collar and stands behind you. Each slave hangs their head in an attitude of subservience, although some are still recovering from being whipped or raped and shudder where they kneel. Other Masters stand behind their slaves and stand so as best to show their muscular physiques, arms folded and shoulders back.

As the results are announced you are amused to glace at the third and second place getters; young, lean slaves almost naked except for leather shorts and G strings, but with heavy collars and, of course, hands cuffed behind them. As the first place is announced you have no idea they are calling your name and that of Master Mark. It is not until Master pulls on your collar, forcing you to stand up that you realize that you had won first prize. As you stand there, bare chest with padlocked nipple thrust forward and balls swinging with their heavy ring, you feel a surge of respect and affection for Masters Mark and Peter, who had brought you to this level of servitude. A plaque reading 'Slave of the Year' is hung around your neck and Master Mark receives an envelope containing cash, which he immediately donates to the local AIDS foundation, to yet more crashing applause.

As the noise subsides Master Mark leads you by the chain down to his table on the floor and pushes you down by his chair, where you sit obediently with your head bowed. He removes the ball gag and puts beer and food in bowls on the floor. You eagerly dig into the food, doggy fashion, and lap up the beer, hardly realizing how hungry and thirsty you were.

For the remainder of the evening you sit at Master Mark's feet and only when most of the crowd has dispersed does he lead you out to the car park again. In a quiet corner of the car park Master Mark hugs and kisses you, saying he is really proud of you and that you are destined to be the best slave he will ever own. He explains that for the rest of the weekend you will be a slave in his house and will go to your own home only on Sunday evening. You should be prepared to be in chains all weekend, to do household chores and to be at his sexual calling, any time of the day or night. You eagerly agree to all of this and feel immensely satisfied that you have been of service to him.

Your cuffed wrists are chained to the grab rail again and your booted ankles clamped to the bike, but the butt plug is left out so the journey back is much more tolerable. The black helmet once again, obscures your hood and gag. Although the streets are almost deserted you catch the occasional look, as someone in a passing car notices your bare arse, handcuffs and shackles on your legs. You wonder if they are truly shocked or, if in fact, envious of your situation. You know where you would rather be, and snuggle closer to Master Mark as he speeds towards his house.

PART 7

As you enter the exclusive outer suburbs you think about your situation. Here you are, handcuffed, hooded and gagged, chained on the back of a motorbike with your arse exposed, cock and weighted balls bouncing on the seat and nipples padlocked. You have spent a great evening as Master Mark's slave and, although you know he is a friend of Master Peter, you have no idea if he will beat the shit out of you, strangle you or otherwise put an end to your life. You pray that your instincts are correct; Master Mark seems powerful but gentle, firm but affectionate and, above all, you have not had any glimmer that he has a nasty streak, and he has had plenty of time to harm you if he wanted to. People had seen you leave the club with him, but who can tell what story he had told them.

The streets become progressively less trafficked, the houses scattered and hidden behind tall brick walls. At the end of one leafy street Master Mark slows to a crawl and stops in front of impressive carved metal gates. They look menacing as he pushes a remote control and they groan as they part. The single track inside the gates is illuminated by lamps in the manicured gardens, beyond which you can see expanses of moonlit lawn and large, established trees. The small, double storied house looms into view and you note the finely crafted wooden latticework and gables over the doors and double glass doors on the front of the house. A garage door opens remotely and Master Mark drives in and parks next to a dark green Jaguar, beyond which you notice an older model Rolls Royce. The cars gleam in the bright garage lights and are clearly objects of great affection. The triple garage space is otherwise home to a variety of tools and boxes, all neatly arranged. The appearance is one of wealth, organization and efficiency.

Master Mark removes your helmet, hood, handcuffs and leg clamps and tells you to kneel on the floor and wait. You cast your eyes to the floor and, with your hands behind you, assume the slaves position, which you have come to know very well. Your weighted balls swing between your legs and beneath your leather jacket you feel your padlocked nipples whenever you move. Although the floor feels hard on your knees you know better than to move or complain.

When Master Mark returns, he attaches a heavy chain to the ball ring and pulls you to your feet.

'Follow me,' he orders and, without any chance for a response, pulls you forward and into the house through an internal door. The heavy chain pulls your balls into the lowest part of your ball sack, but you dare not touch them. Instead you keep you hands behind your back.

Through an inconspicuous door Master leads you down a wooden staircase to a basement, dimly illuminated by a couple of wall lights. Within a short while you realize this was the dungeon that Master Peter had told you about. In one corner a St Andrew's Cross is pivoted on a large, central bolt, with multiple straps along each limb. A small metal cage is in another corner. From the ceiling hang a variety of chains and ropes, including chains with metal neck collars attached. The walls are lined with all manner of bondage equipment, such as in a BDSM store. A metal frame dominates the centre of the dungeon. From each corner of the frame hang chains and handcuffs and a rope noose hangs from the centre of the top bar. To one side a rubber, padded table has fixation points around its edges and a central hole for arse or cock and ball work. Hanging in one corner are a variety of hoods, collars, gags, leather and rubber clothing, whips and paddles. You notice a small bathroom off to one side.

Without ceremony Master Mark pulls you to the floor and padlocks the chain to a bolt in the floor, forcing your legs apart and your balls to within a few inches of the floor. He quickly pulls a tight rubber hood over your head. There are pinholes over the eyes and the mouth hole is filled with a ball gag, which Master ties tightly behind your head. You feel the collar tighten and then a click as a further padlock ensures the hood will not be removed. Master removes your leather jacket and deftly applies rigid handcuffs, which prevent any movement of your hands behind your back. He applies leather cuffs to your elbows and pulls them firmly together behind your back.

You squat there, fixed by your ball ring to the floor, hooded, gagged, with your elbows and wrists firmly anchored behind your back. After a few moments you feel Master apply chains to your padlocked nipples. Nobody had touched your nipples since they were pierced and the padlocks locked into places some eight days before. There is no pain, just a pulling sensation as chains are lifted up and attached to some point in the ceiling. Any movement downwards, however, results in pain in your nipples and any movement upwards cause your balls to be painfully stretched. You groan with satisfaction as you settle into your new slave position. Although you cannot see anything that is not immediately in front of you, you detect that Master has left the dungeon and you hear his booted feet on the stairs up to the house.

The dim light in the dungeon enables you to fix your limited vision on the equipment around you. Although you are naked, you are not cold. The dungeon is heated via ceiling ducts, and every now and then you hear a distant heater turn on. The tiles on the floor are old and cracked, but clean and you smell a faint aroma of disinfectant. The equipment and dungeon appears well used, but clean and well maintained. This scene gives you confidence that this Master is experienced, careful and likely to take care of his slaves, as well as he does his property.

You hear thumping around in the main house above you as Master moves from room to room. You hear water running as Master has a shower, then more thumping as he replaces his boots and moves around the house again. You estimate you have been chained up for an hour before you hear Master's footsteps on the dungeon stairs. Without ceremony Master Mark unchains your padlocked nipples and ball ring and pulls you to your feet. He attaches a chain to your rigid handcuffs and pulls it over a ceiling beam. As he pulls on the chain your arms are raised painfully behind your back. With the hood and gag in place you can only grunt and gasp. As your arms are raised up, your head is thrust forwards and when Master attaches another chain to the front of your collar and pulls it to the bolthole in the floor, you are fixed in position. As a final gesture to fixing you in position, Master attaches leather cuffs to each ankle and fixes them wide apart via chains to more bolt holes in the floor. You can neither move upwards nor downwards, to the right nor to the left.

In this position your arse feels completely exposed and your balls hang down, weighted by the ring. You feel Master's hands caressing your buttocks and balls and stroking your rigid cock. This causes spasms of erotic tension and you to strain against your arms and neck, sending your weighted balls swinging. Master slowly enters your arse with his fingers and smears lubricant around and inside your hole. You feel him enter with one, two, three fingers and stretch your arse by flexing his fingers and moving them in and out repeatedly. You then feel him grasp your waist and fix you onto his erect cock, which he slowly works inside you. He thrusts deeper and deeper until the whole shaft is buried in your arse. Slowly he pumps away, sometimes playing around the entrance, sometimes thrusting up to his pubic hairs, at which stage you feel his leather clad legs bang against your buttocks. He takes delight in varying his thrusting motion, sometimes shallow, sometimes deep, sometime moving in a circular motion, so you never know what to expect. The whole scene has you trembling with excitement and your cock is oozing pre cum onto the tiled floor. Movement is impossible and you are able only to groan.

Eventually Master makes a series of deep lunges and holds himself deep inside you as you feel the warm rush of semen fill his condom. He holds himself there for what seems like an eternity, before pulling out. You hear him remove the condom and then feel the caress of a towel, as he wipes your arse. He continues to play with your arse and after a short while you feel your arse stretching again as he inserts a butt plug. The plug is larger than his cock and you groan and buck as he pushes past the widest part of the plug. With a groan of relieve you feel your muscles clamp around the narrow base. Master ties a rope around your waist then between your legs to fasten the butt plug in place.

By this time your arms are aching and your neck is sore from being pulled down to the floor. Master releases the hand and elbow cuffs, unties your ankles and releases the chain around your neck, which enables you to stand upright again. With the hood and gag still in place you sigh with relief and massage some life back into your wrists and hands, before a smart whack on your arse with a whip brings you to your senses. How could you have thought to do something without permission? You quickly bring your hands behind your back, in the slave's position, and bow your hooded head in submission.

'That's better,' Master Mark growls as he pushes you forwards towards the St Andrew's Cross, dragging the chain attached to your ball ring behind you.

He turns you so that your back is to the cross, then lifts your legs onto the footrests. He quickly fastens the straps around your legs and arms, then three straps across your chest and abdomen and one around each upper thigh. You are unable to move. Master fastens the collar to another bolthole before removing the gag. The fresh air is so sweat as you clear the spit from your mouth and lick your lips.

'Thank you Sir,' is all you can say, but the relief is real.

The chain, still hanging from your balls, is looped and tied so that it hangs only a short length from your ball ring. The weight however, ensures that your balls are forced to the deepest part of the sac.

Without warning Master starts to turn the cross like the hand on a clock. When you are horizontal the heavy chain wrenches you balls sideways, and as you open your mouth to gasp, Master thrusts his erect cock into it. Because your neck is fixed to the frame you cannot avoid the thrusting cock.

'Suck it boy and don't bite.'

You open your mouth as wide as it will go in order to accommodate Master's huge member. You taste the condom which Master said he would use, at least until he knows you and your habits a little more. You wonder how Master manages to maintain his erection, having just cum in your arse, but he has no trouble maintaining a rock hard cock. As he thrusts deeper and deeper you gag and feel spit come into your mouth, to lubricate Master's cock even more. You feel powerless; hooded, plugged and tied to the cross; you have no control over your body. The pain from your stretched balls and the plug in your arse ensure you do not loose your own erection.

Master pounds your mouth mercilessly. As your jaws begin to ache you can no longer keep your mouth open, and in a flash Master withdraws and slaps you on the dick as he feels your teeth on his cock. Immediately he forces your mouth open again and inserts an O-ring gag, which keeps your teeth well apart. He ties the straps tightly behind your head so there is no chance of your jaws coming together again. He resumes fucking your mouth, and you periodically gag when his dick hits the back of your throat. This seems to excite Master even more. The collar anchors your head so you have no way to avoid the onslaught. With one heave he thrusts into the very depths of your throat and you feel him shudder as he spurts yet another load.

Without ceremony. Master Mark withdraws his cock and straightens the cross so that you are once again positioned vertical. The chain now pulls your balls painfully downwards but at least your feet rest on the footrests and the pressure from the straps is relieved on your arms and legs. Master unties the O-ring gag and replaces it with a bit gag. Even on top of the mask the gag pulls painfully at the corners of your mouth as Master tightens the straps, before going back upstairs into the house.

The dim light is poor company and only enables you to focus your limited vision on the other items of torture in the dungeon. As time passes your mind turns over the events of the past 24 hours; the humiliation at the club, the near naked ride, the abuse in the dungeon, and all the time your body has been the property of Master Mark. He had ensured you had no control of it by constantly keeping it exposed, cuffed and bound, and by making sure you had no say in events by keeping you gagged and hooded. Here you are, plugged, gagged, hooded and bound to the cross. Slave heaven, you think, and your erect cock and balls ache for release.

It seems like hours before you realize that there is no movement in the house above you. You strain to listen but silence is all that surrounds you. You realize that Master has gone to sleep, leaving you tied to the cross. More hours pass and you eventually doze off. The night passes and you are intermittently woken by pain in your arse, as your muscles relax and the plug moves slightly downwards, forcing the wider part of the plug to stretch your arse. Each time you wake you gasp for air as your head has slumped forwards and the collar threatens to cut off your breathing. Each time you force yourself to regulate your breathing and calm down. Spit dribbles from around the bit gag. You can no longer hold your piss and you groan with relief as you piss onto the tiled floor; a small moment of pleasure when all around you is pain.

Eventually your arms become quite numb, and whilst you can move your fingers, you noticed that there is no feeling in them. Your legs seem OK, notwithstanding the tight straps which anchor them to the cross.

More time passes. Eventually you hear the dawn chorus in the garden and, through a chink in the blacked windows, you notice daylight. Banging on the floors above you indicates that Master is awake and shortly he comes down the stairs, naked. Firstly he removes the bit gag and hood and you gasp as the cool, fresh air hits your face. He then removes the chain from your balls and all the straps, which secure you to the cross. In the end you are fixed only by your neck collar, and as he releases this, you slump forwards over his shoulders. You realize you have lost all power in your arms and legs. As Master lowers you into the pool of piss on the floor you struggle randomly to get some circulation moving. On the cold tiles sensation slowly returns but it is another 10 minutes before you can stand without falling over.

Wearing only the ball weight and butt plug, Master leads you into the bathroom and instructs you to remove the plug then take a shower. You sit on the toilet and release the rope fixing the plug in place. Surprisingly, the plug does not fall out but you have to force it out, eventually pulling on it from below. An explosion of shit and air follows and you are grateful for the release. Master Mark stands over you with his arms folded. He says he wants to piss and without more ado proceeds to piss over you, saturating your head and with rivulets of piss running around your body and onto the floor and toilet. He then leaves silently.

The shower feels so good. Warm and cleansing it helps ease the aches out of your muscles and enables you to clean the dried sweat and piss from your skin. You dare not linger around your cock and balls with the soap as you feel an erection start whenever you go near them. Since Master does not return, you dry yourself. You decide you had better clean the piss off the bathroom and dungeon floors, or you imagine he will have you lick it up.

Just as you finish wiping the floors you are startled by the sound of boots on floorboards, laughter and chairs scraping.

PART 8

The sounds from the house above suggest that Master Mark is not alone. You hear several voices, one of which you recognize as that of Master Peter. You are pleased that Master Peter is in the group; he is someone who treats you firmly, but with respect and you know you will come to no harm while he is around. You do not recognize the third voice, a deep resonant voice with a European accent. You suspect the third person is German, and you remember that both Masters Peter and Mark have spent several holidays trawling the leather bars of Berlin and Hamburg.

You finish cleaning up. Master Mark has not given any instructions to you, so you decide to tidy up the towels, ropes, chains and condoms, which litter the dungeon and attest to last nights activities. You clean the ropes and chains with water and wipe the leather straps on the cross with leather cleaner. Having cleaned and tidied everything you kneel on the floor with your hands behind your back and await further developments.

Shortly you hear boots on the floor above. People are talking and laughing as they make their way down the steps to the dungeon. With your eyes cast down all you can see are three pairs of boots before you. You recognize Master Mark's tall boots from the evening before and Master Peter's army boots have their characteristic shine to them. The third pair of boots are black cowboy boots, over tight, black, leather pants.

'That's a good boy. I like a slave who cleans up his mess without being prompted. It shows that the slave knows his place as the domestic slut he is,' said Master Mark.

'Yeah, he's learning fast. Soon he'll be useful as a slave for hiring out to Masters around town. Some of them are real dirty pigs and he we can earn a fortune hiring him out to clean up their stinking mess,' said Master Peter.

'He can start by cleaning my dungeon,' the new voice says quickly. 'Of course he will need to wear my slave shackles, but I guess he'll manage. I'll just chain him to the wall until you can come and collect him.'

You are intrigued by the newcomer. He has a deep, sonorous voice and, despite the accent, is clearly well educated. You know that Peter and Mark have several wealthy friends, and hope this man is one of them.

'OK boy, here's the deal.' Master Peter is taking charge.

'You've come a long way in the past few months. Each weekend you've been subjected to severe and prolonged bondage and torture. You've been fucked in every hole, usually several times a night, without complaint. You've obeyed our instructions without question and without us having to the beat the shit out of you, except when it pleased us. Several of our friends have commented on how lucky we are and whilst we have shared you with some of them, we do not trust all of them and will protect you from them. Our new friend here, Ian, is from Germany and has invited us to his place in the forest.'

Your mind is spinning. You dare not look up without permission but you are dying to glance at this new Master. Instead you keep your eyes on the boots in front of you and your hands behind your back.

'How does that sound boy?'

'Thank you Sir. I'd like that very much,' you reply.

'This is no weekend trip boy. We plan to be away for a long time, maybe several months. Can you manage that?'

'Yes Sir. I think I can take leave from my job.' You know that with your boss's connections to the leather scene, he will be well informed of your plans and will not object.

Master Ian speaks and immediately you are aroused. 'OK, this is what will happen. You fly to Germany next month. For the journey you will wear a rubber butt plug, held in place with tight leather ropes. You will wear a rubber cock and ball ring. These devices will be put on you shortly before you go to the airport and after you've cleaned yourself out. On arrival in Germany you will immediately be locked into metal shackles and chains, and these will be welded into position. OK?'

'Yes Sir,' you reply.

'Today however, we have an extra treat in store for you,' Master Ian says. 'Look at me when I speak to you.'

Without hesitation you raise your head and stare at Master Ian. He is the tallest of all present, well over six feet. His muscular body is tightly encased in leather chaps and a shirt. His cock and balls swing freely and you gasp at the sight of the huge PA ring in his cock. You had always wanted one of these but had not had the courage to go for it. A black leather cap sits awkwardly on his blond hair. His face is framed with a short beard, and you guess he is in his thirties.

Without ceremony, Master Ian pulls you to your feet and backs you up to the pole in the middle of the dungeon. He quickly cuffs your wrists behind the pole and ties your ankles to the sides of the pole with rope. Several more ropes are used to secure your chest and belly to the pole and a rope around your neck ensures that you will not move your head. The ropes around your chest spare your padlocked nipples. If anything they are thrust forwards by the pressure of the ropes. Master Mark adds a wide ball gag and ties it tightly in place.

Master Ian brings in a table and unwraps a bunch of sterile surgical instruments. You gasp into your gag and the sweat starts to run down your arms and legs. Your mind is working overtime wondering what these three Masters have in mind. All three are donning sterile gloves and busy doing things with small packages. Amongst the paraphernalia you notice a large PA ring and a couple of large nipple rings.

Master Peter produces a small key and proceeds to unlock the padlocks in your nipples. This is the first time they have been removed since being placed there several months ago. There is no pain as the padlocks are removed but you wince and squirm as he forces the much larger nipple rings through the holes. The holes created by the padlocks guide the rings and Master's deft hands ensure that no flesh is torn. The extra wide rings do, however, stretch the holes and it is some minutes before this searing pain subsides. Using pliers, Master Peter ensures that the ball is fixed between the open ends of the ring. There is no chance these could be removed without considerable effort.

You gasp through the ball gag and sweat pours down your face as your new nipple rings are inserted. Had you not been fixed to the pole you feel you might have passed out.

'Well done boy,' says Master Peter, as he dabs your nipples with soothing oil and massages it into the holes. 'That's you ringed for the future.'

Master Ian takes over and starts by washing your cock with a blue sterilizing solution. Squirm as you do you cannot avoid the inevitable. You are terrified of what is going to happen and whilst you had always wanted a PA ring, you imagined you would have had it inserted under an anaesthetic. Spit dribbles from around the ball gag and sweat pours down your belly and onto your ball ring, dripping onto the floor. Master Mark grabs and steadies your cock, opening up the piss hole at the same time. Although the rope around you neck prevents you looking down you can sense what is happening. Master Mark drips a soothing gel into your piss hole and massages it into the hole and around the outside. You suspect this is an anaesthetic, but prepare yourself for the worst anyway.

After five minutes, Master Ian returns holding a large needle with a plastic sheath. You have not seen such large needles before and groan into your gag. Master Peter holds a bottle of amyl to your nose and you take several deep breaths before you start to relax, only to lurch awake and scream into the gag as Master Ian thrust the needle through your piss hole and out the back of your cock. You have never known such pain. It feels as though your cock is being nailed to a cross. Even your balls ache as the shear terror of the ordeal causes your ball sac to contract against the heavy ball ring.

Master Ian works on regardless of your grunting and squirming. He removes the needle, leaving the plastic sheath in place, then places the end of the PA ring in the sheath and pulls it through the hole. There is no further pain, just more pushing and pulling. He screws the ball into the open end of the PA and lets it hang down. As he steps backwards you notice that there is no blood on his hands. From the amount of pain you had experienced you had expected there to be blood everywhere. All Masters mumble amongst themselves, showing no concern that you were in any danger. This gives you confidence that what they have done is successful.

It is five minutes before you regulate your breathing. The tears that run down your face merge with the sweat on you body and dry to salty streaks. You forget altogether about the pain in your nipples; the dull throbbing in your cock commands all your attention.

'OK boy, that's it. You're ringed and PA'd and ready to travel. The PA will take a couple of weeks to settle down so don't fiddle with it; just wash it with soap and water when you are in the shower. We went straight for the large size so you won't need it replacing,' says Master Ian, with the authority of an expert.

The gag and bonds are removed and you slump onto Master Peter, who lowers you gently to sit on the floor. You stare at your new piercings. The nipple rings are thick and heavy. The PA is a size zero and weighs your cock down. When you stand up it causes jabs of pain as it bangs against your ball ring. Immediately your see it, you start to get an erection. You have not seen anything so erotic before and you are glad of this final act, confirming your role as a slave.

'Now boy, how are you going to thank your Masters?' says Master Peter with a sneer. His erect cock suggests that no answer is really necessary.

Within seconds you are collared, on your knees again and cuffed with hands behind the pole. Your feet are tied behind the pole and the collar anchored in place so that your head is immobile once again. You know what is coming and open your mouth expectantly. Being fucked in the mouth seems a small discomfort after what you have just been through.

One after the other your three Masters take advantage of your open and willing mouth. When not fucking your face they suck each other's cocks, so that eventually all three shoot their loads over you. This is the ultimate humiliation for you - cuffed, collared, tied, ringed and PA'd and being used as a fuck / suck slave. You relish your position and your erect cock with its PA serves to demonstrate your joy.

You are released from the pole and allowed to shower. Your street clothes are in a bag and you put them on, carefully so as not to knock your new piercings. There is no escape, however, from the pressure of your tight jeans on the PA and you walk very carefully to avoid further rubbing. Your Masters have prepared a meal and in the later afternoon they sit at a table to eat, whilst you eat like a dog, from a bowl on the floor.

The Masters discuss arrangements for the upcoming trip and, having received your agreement, do not involve you in the discussion further, other than to allow you to overhear the conversation. A departure date is fixed for some six weeks in the future and you are instructed to make arrangements for a long stay overseas. This only means locking the door of your apartment and making sure your mail is diverted.

At the end of the day, and with your new piercings starting to ache and throb, you catch a taxi home. You contemplate the upcoming trip. The Masters told you not to bring any baggage other than a set of travel clothes. The thought of what this meant sends spasms of pain through your cock again as it strains with its PA against your jeans.

PART 9

The next six weeks drag by. At work you are pleased that your boss had no objection to your being absent for a long spell. You know your boss has links with the leather community and you suspect he is fully informed by your Masters of the plans for the trip. You even wonder how active your boss is in the leather scene, when you see him hoon into the car park on his Harley, complete with leather pants and jacket and knee high boots. Of course, by the time he reaches his office he is the epitome of the city financier, with tailored suit and smart shoes. Occasionally you catch his eye and detect a secret grin, but nothing is ever said and you are grateful he allows you to get on with your work. Through his guidance you have achieved huge profits for the company and it is this, along with your obvious dedication to the company, that enables you to take some time off.

You organize things at the office so that your absence will not affect your clients. At the end of the day you are happy that you have made all the right decisions and there will be no problem when you return. In the evenings you can think of nothing but your trip, the bondage / slavery trip of a lifetime.

Within a few days of their insertion, the nipple rings cease to ache, except when you knock them. Your PA is remarkably pain free, unless you play with your cock. The large PA weighs your cock between your legs, until you get an erection, but it is some weeks before you can massage it without feeling as though your cock has flames coming from it.

A week before your departure you receive your ticket and a set of instructions from Master Peter. You are to travel on the same plane, but he and Master Mark will be in business class while you will be in economy. You think the journey will take a couple of hours only, so this does not bother you too much. Your dietary instructions are much the same as before. You are to stop eating anything 3 days before departure, other than the high protein, high calorie drink you had used in the past. This means that within a day your stomach is empty and with a few douches on the day of departure, you are perfectly clean inside.

You get your apartment in order, divert your mail and stop all deliveries. Three days before departure you receive a package in the mail from Master Peter, which contains a medium sized rubber butt plug and a rubber cock and ball ring. You understand that anything metal will set off the detectors at the airport, so you are grateful that these are solid rubber. You practice inserting and tying in the butt plug so that it will not fall out. The cock and ball ring keep your cock erect and your balls pulled tightly into their sacs. Your PA strains at the tip of your cock and it takes a lot of pushing to get the whole works into your jocks and tight jeans. Your cock is plainly outlined through the faded and worn jeans. The whole arrangement is as hot as hell, without actually being naked. You practice walking and sitting with the plug and ball rings in place, and whilst there is no problem for a short period, after 20 minutes your arse is aching and you are squirming to relieve the pressure in your cock and balls.

The instructions also call for you to wear a white sweatshirt and boots. You can wear your leather jacket if it is cold. The only things you pack in your carry-on bag are some toiletries and a spare pair of jocks.

On the day of departure you meet Masters Peter and Mark at the airport. By this time you had had the butt plug in for an hour and it is already making your arse ache. Your cock and balls are straining against their rubber rings and bulge from the front of your jeans, obvious to anyone who glanced between your legs. Masters are delighted with the effect and at your obvious discomfort. You receive more than a few stares from the airline check-in guys, one of whom offers to up-grade you, but you think better of disobeying Masters' instructions.

Your two Masters are dressed in casual clothes but you notice them checking in four heavy suitcases, which you suspect are not full of beachwear. Masters' boots alone would take one suitcase and they have a dungeon full of gear at home.

You all hang around in the departure lounge, and shortly before boarding you think to empty your bladder so as not to have to go to the toilet on the plane, with associated parading of yourself in front of the other passengers. You lock yourself in a cubicle and open your fly. Your engorged cock bursts out, relieved to be free of the constricting jeans. Piss goes everywhere but in the bowl; there is no way you can point your cock down and the PA ring ensures maximum spray. You feel the butt plug, which is firmly tied in place, and give the rope an extra hitch to make sure the plug will not fall out. After much heaving and pushing you get your cock back in your jeans and return to the lounge. Masters are pleased with the drop of precum that is staining your jeans. This serves to demonstrate the PA, which is perfectly outlined now.

Blushing with embarrassment you make your way to the back of the plane and gently lower yourself onto the seat, covering your legs with a pillow. Whilst the seat is soft, you know that after an hour it will be like a plank. You feel the butt plug being forced against the wide flange and into your arse another inch. This is just enough to stretch your arse to your limit and you grit your teeth as you fasten your seat belt. Things are not too bad while the plane is stationary but as it starts to judder on take off, and at every lurch due to turbulence, the plug shoots spasms of pain into your arse. You grip the armrests, praying for the plane to be still. Each movement sends the plug further into your arse, and massages another drop of fluid from your prostate and onto your jeans.

Mercifully you do not need to visit the toilet during the flight, but you avoid drinking anything just in case. You try reading, but the pain in your arse and the throbbing of your engorged cock refocuses your mind on the mission at hand. It seems that your period as a bound slave starts a long time before you arrive in Germany.

Landing is particularly uncomfortable and you try to ease the pressure in your arse by pushing up slightly on the armrests. It works to a degree but you have to sit on the plug eventually. What a relief as you stand to exit the plane, holding your leather jacket in front on the wet patch on your jeans. It is warm outside so you hold your jacket in place, until it is whipped away by Master Mark in the terminal. You receive more stares at your bulge and the growing wet stain, outlining your PA. Quickly the bags arrive and you all go outside, where you are met by Master Ian.

The specific arrangements have been kept from you. You know you are to be kept as a bondage slave, although no period has been specified. You have arranged a couple of months off work, just in case the Masters have some long-term ideas. Master Ian is semi-retired but you know that Masters Peter and Mark have work to go back to. Whatever the duration, the thought of this long period as a slave, rather than the usual night or long weekend, is sure to have a lasting impression on you. Already you live for your next bondage / slavery session, with whomever of your two Masters wants you. Your whole life is focused on being a slave. This curiously enhances your work, as you no longer dread another boring weekend, hanging around bars and street corners, hoping for more than the usual quick fuck. You know that sessions with Masters Peter and Mark are full on, leather and bondage, no holes barred, all night or weekend affairs, sometimes with other Masters, sometimes in isolated rural locations and always with you completely at their mercy.

Master Ian is dressed in tight jeans, boots and a black sweatshirt and leather jacket. He looks every bit the leather Master. His muscular body, towering above everyone else, draws more than a few stares. Dragging your Masters' bags you all walk through the car park and stop at a black, windowless kombi van. You put the bags in the back then climb in after them. Master Ian gets in the drivers seat and Masters Peter and Mark get into the back with you. Master Ian gives instructions from the front seat, that all the gear Masters Peter and Mark will need is in the wooden box at the base of the pole.

You are told to strip, which you do, relieved that you can release your engorged cock and balls. You fold your clothes and kneel with hands behind your back, eyes cast down to the floor, like a good slave. You are instructed to remove your butt plug and cock and ball rings, which you do. You slide the butt plug out slowly, and are relieved that only a small amount of mucous follows the plug, and this is easily wiped away. The relief causes you to sigh, which earns you a slap on the dick.

'Shut up boy and bend over,' says Master Peter, as he pushes your head down onto the floor.

He opens your legs wide and you know what is going to happen. Without discussion he massages more lubricant into your arse and you catch a glimpse of a cone shaped butt plug tapering to a narrow neck, but much wider than anything you have experienced in the past. It requires all your concentration to remain silent, to breathe deeply and to relax your arse, which is already tender from the rubber plug. Master Peter slowly pushes the plug in until it reaches the widest part. You are beside yourself with pain and try as you might, you cannot relax any more. Master Mark produces some amyl and after a few whiffs you feel a little more relaxed. After some hefty pushing and twisting the plug sinks in, and your arse tightens around the narrow neck. Although there is no chance this will fall out, chains are threaded through a loop in the base plate and around your balls and cock, to be tightened and padlocked to a leather belt that is locked around your waist. Chains also pass up your arse crack and are padlocked to the belt at the back.

You are then instructed to stand up and hold onto the bars on the roof of the van. The weight of the butt plug is immediately obvious when you stand up, and you are glad of the fixing chains. Your legs are spread again and a heavy ball ring fixed in place so that your balls are, once again, forced into the bottom of the ball sac. You put your hands down and a thick leather hood is placed over your head. There are holes for your nose but no eyeholes. The hood is tied tightly at the back. A pecker gag is fixed over the hood and further straps fix the hood in place across your eyes, under your chin, and of course, around your neck. You hear padlocks securing each of these straps and know that the hood will not be removed for a long time.

You are manoeuvred back towards the pole, which is cold against your back. Your hands are pulled behind the pole and, with your wrists parallel tied tightly. Your elbows are similarly pulled back and tied behind the post. Further rope is added to your arms and around your chest and belly so that you are firmly fixed to the pole. Ropes then tie your ankles, knees and thighs to the pole so that movement in any direction is impossible. A padlock secures your collar to the pole. Although you are tightly tied to the pole, the only discomfort you feel is from the butt plug in your arse.

Suddenly you feel searing pain in you right then left nipple as a chain is padlocked between your nipple rings. A weight is attached to your ball ring which further pulls your balls downwards into their sac. Your cock, which until then had been erect, begins to deflate as you focus on the pain in your nipples. As you begin to wonder what more they could do, you feel someone washing your cock and massaging lubricant into the piss hole. You had been catheterized before so you knew what to expect. Slowly the catheter is pushed in and, squirm as you might, you cannot escape it. After a sudden urge to piss, the catheter is in, and the balloon inflated so that it will not fall out. A bag is attached to the end and tied to your left leg. You know this indicates a long journey.

Hooded, gagged, collared, pierced, plugged, catheterized and tied tightly to a pole you wonder what you have let yourself in for. As your mind wanders you to feel the Masters pull a heavy canvas sack over you, tying it at the top and bottom and around your neck. A hole for your nose enables you to breathe, but nothing else. More ropes tie the canvas bag in place so that you are disguised as a sack and hardly recognizable as the bound slave you are.

You hear doors opening and closing and shortly the van starts its journey. You have no sense of direction and can only detect sharp corners when your rope bonds pull against you. Your ball weights bounce around painfully and the nipple chain pulls down sharply whenever you hit a bump in the road. But on and on the van goes. You hear muffled talk and laughter, but your Masters seem unconcerned about their bound cargo in the back.

After what seems like a couple of hours the van stops. From the sounds and smells you guess this is a service station, and shortly you hear the fuel cap come off and the sound of fuel being pumped. Some idle chatter outside the van reaches you as a muffled hum and shortly, the van sets off again.

The van pulls up after a short distance and you hear the sound of doors locking. Then nothing. You are alone, tied and gagged in the back of a van, in the middle of Germany, on the way to god only knows where. You are scared, but excited and if being like this was what being a slave is all about, you want more of it.

Just as you are beginning to wonder if the Masters are ever coming back, you hear the doors open and close. Someone is removing the canvas bag and untying you from the pole, only to retie the ropes around you, but leaving you standing free. Your arms are still tied tightly behind your back, even more so now that the pole is not there. The chain between your nipple rings is removed. You are lowered to the floor on your front, care being taken to move your catheter and weighted balls between your legs. Your ankles are then drawn up and tied to your wrists, making a hog tie of you. The canvas bag is put over you again, leaving your head free but tied tightly around the rest of you. You are then fixed to the floor with ropes across your back and legs, but leaving your neck free.

You feel someone put a cushion under your head, but this kindness was not to last for long, as shortly someone sits on the cushion, pushing their naked body against your hooded head. Your gag is removed and, before you can take a deep breath, a large O-ring is tied into your mouth, stretching your mouth wide open. An erect cock is forced into your open mouth. In your hog tie and being strapped to the floor you cannot move anywhere to avoid the cock; only some slight up and down movement is possible, but as the Master settles down he takes control of your hooded head and manoeuvres it as he wants. There is nothing you can do but take the cock in your mouth.

As he van takes off again your head is pounded up and down onto the cock. When the road is smooth, the Master forces his cock into the back of your throat so that you gag. Every 20 minutes the Masters change places and once the van stops, so the driver can come back to fuck you in the mouth. All the time your cock is straining against the floor of the van. You settle into the pattern of bouncing up and down with a cock in your mouth, and mostly you enjoy every minute of it. Occasionally the van goes over a bump in the road and the cock is forced deep down your throat, causing you to gag and heave. After an hour the road is very bumpy and you suspect you are on a bush track. Even the Master finds the constant pounding too much and removes his cock, leaving you to dribble on the floor, but at least you are able to take some deep breaths.

After a further 10 minutes the van lurches to a stop and, without a word, the Masters leave the van. Silence is all around you, the hood effectively stopping any but the loudest noises in. You concentrate on your butt plug, the catheter, your ball ring and your erect cock, which mercifully starts to deflate. Your jaws ache from the relentless face fucking, and the O-ring. After what seems a life time the back of the van opens and your bonds are removed, leaving you with the butt plug, catheter, ball ring, and the hood is still firmly strapped to your head. You are led by a chain attached to your collar out of the van, across some grass and into what you presume is a barn of some sort; the smell of hay and cow shit are clues. You are forced into a kneeling position and the hood and O-ring are removed. The wave of fresh air on your face causes you to sway but Master Ian steadies you by holding you firmly against his leather-covered thighs.

You are offered a bottle of fruit juice, then another, and you gulp them to quench your burning thirst. You notice very little urine coming from the catheter and remember you had not drunk since the morning, and it is now late afternoon. You notice at one end of the barn a brazier with a roaring fire in it and several chains and shackles slung around. Without ceremony, Master Ian pushes you towards the fire and forces you once again to your knees. Master Mark holds a wide metal collar ready and encircles your neck with it, locking it at the front with a key. The collar fits snugly around your neck so that it does not rub when you move your head. Next, snug metal shackles connected by short chains are attached to your wrists and ankles and locked in place. A long chain is attached to the collar, down to the wrist chain then down to the ankle chain. Each free end of the chain is padlocked to its metal cuff around your neck, wrists and ankles. Only a minimum of movement is possible. Your wrists are held at mid belly level, so there is no chance of you playing with yourself. Master Peter takes over with a red hot metal rod and welds the collar, wrist and ankle shackles shut. You are now permanently collared and shackled, or at least until someone cuts them off. As you try to move around you realize how heavy the shackles and chains are, and nothing but a shuffle is possible.

'We hope you like your new clothes boy, because that's all you will be wearing while you are here.'

No answer seems necessary and you are still getting your mind around the permanency of this bondage. You had not experienced anything like it before and it added a whole new dimension to your slavery. Your cock is hard, pointing your PA up and pulling your balls painfully against their metal ring.

You are led back to a stable and told to lie down on the hay. A rough blanket is thrown over you and you are told to get some sleep. As you lay there you can see that the Masters had thought that, with the catheter, you will not need to take a piss, and the plug keeps your arse closed. The hay is at least soft, if not comfortable, and you settle down to a fitful sleep. You wake periodically when the cold metal chain rubs against your PA, or the butt plug works its way to its widest part, then stops as your arse stretches painfully.

The long night ends abruptly as the blanket is ripped away and a bucket of cold water thrown over you.

PART 10

'Get up boy, you've got work to do,' Master Mark shouts, as he hauls you to your feet.

Pulling you to a shower at the side of the house, he lets the cold water run over you before he washes you with a sponge. You move as best you can in your shackles and chains, to enable him to wash you properly. During the shower Master Mark removes your butt plug and washes out your arse. When the catheter comes out you feel a sting and the urgency to piss but, of course, your bladder is empty and nothing comes out.

Still wet, you are pulled by a chain attached to your collar into the house. The other two Masters are sitting at a table eating breakfast and you are told to drink your protein mixture, which is in a bowl on the floor. You struggle to your knees and gratefully lap up the mixture, which is to be your staple diet. Master Ian refills the bowl and you suck and lap more fluid until you feel full. He then drags and pushes you on your knees until you are under the table where the Masters are eating.

'OK boy, service us,' he says.

You realize, when you look up, that they are all wearing chaps, with cock and balls free. You know what is required of you.

As you advance between Master Peter's legs, he opens them to let you take his condom-covered cock in your mouth. He slides down the chair slightly to enable the full length of his erect cock to penetrate to the back of your throat. You had learned to suck cock whilst cuffed or tied up, so this was not difficult. Up and down you go, feeling the cock grow harder and harder until he finally bucks upwards, fixing your head against the underside of the table, and blows his load.

Without interrupting the conversation between the Masters, you shuffle round under the table to service the other two Masters. Only Master Ian takes control by grabbing your head under the table and forcing his cock down your throat, but Master Mark is happy to have you do all the work.

'Clean up,' shouts Master Ian as they all leave the table. You shuffle out from under table and work out how best to clear up the breakfast mess. The kitchen is small, but it takes forever to shuffle around in your shackles and move all the stuff into the cupboards and wash the crockery. At the end you go to the middle of the kitchen and kneel on the floor with your head bowed and wait for further instructions.

After half an hour, and just as your knees are going numb on the stone floor, the three Masters come into the kitchen and sit down around you. You continue to stare at the floor. Master Ian speaks.

'This is how it will be boy. You are now an official slave. Because of your performance in your own country, we have registered you as a slave here in Germany. You have an official entry in the National Register of Slaves, which is available to a select number of Masters who have proven themselves trustworthy. Your number is120448 and this is engraved on your collar. Your life will be one of absolute servitude for as long as you are here. We have checked out all the Masters who will use and abuse you. They are all safe and healthy and will not do anything you have not experienced already. Their integrity in the leather world depends on their behaviour towards slaves, and if any Master transgresses the code of conduct, they may find themselves in your position. The National Register of Masters maintains very high standards for its members and they monitor their behaviour very closely. All complaints are followed up by thorough investigation.

During the daytime you will be abused by us and any of our friends who visit. You will be shackled and tied up the whole time. At night your chains will be removed but not the metal collar and cuffs, which are welded into position. The metal ball ring is also locked in place and only I have the key. You will be dressed in leather pants, boots and jacket and a hood will be tightly laced onto you head. The eyeholes are open but the hood has an integral gag. Your hands will be padlocked behind you and a chain leash attached to your metal collar. You will then be taken to the 'slaves corner'. This is a road junction in the leather quarter of town where registered slaves are handcuffed to posts and there await their Master for the night.

Only the appointed Master has the key to your padlocked wrists, so whilst others may try to take you, only the registered Master will have the correct key. You may have to wait an hour for him. He may not turn up at all, in which case you will be handcuffed to the post all night and we will collect you in the morning. We, of course, will be enjoying ourselves with other slaves who are booked for us.

So while we will not be able to keep an eye on you, you can be sure that the Masters who will own you for the night are all reliable. They have been rigorously screened and if there are any reports of unsafe practices they are 'arrested' and investigated. Punishment is removal from the Masters' register, and the only way they can be readmitted to the register is for them to be slaves themselves for a week. You may see them on the street corner. They are usually naked and gagged and hogtied to the posts. People can then abuse them as they want for the evening. Mostly leathermen and slaves alike come out of the leather bars and piss on them. At midnight they are released and find their way home. Each night for a week they come back to the post and ask to be tied up again. Only after they have endured the seven nights, and promise to behave themselves, are they readmitted to the Masters' register. Some, of course, find that being a slave suits them, and start their nights tied to the post, as you will, to be taken by appointed Masters.

We hope this is all clear to you boy. Any questions?'

Your head is spinning from this information. Can it really be that you will be used by a different Master each night, and in the day time return to your three Masters here, to be abused at their will. It all sounds too good to be true.

'No Sir. Thank you for this experience,' you offer as a gesture of your gratitude.

'To start with we are having a few friends over for lunch. Expect some action,' Master Ian says definitively.

He extracts keys from his pocket and proceeds to unlock your chains. You feel as though you are floating without the weight of the heavy chains pulling on your neck and wrists. Master Peter then takes over and with Master Mark's help pushes you towards a padded bench, over which you are flexed. The cross beam of the bench is in your stomach and your head and arms hang over the other side. Chains are rapidly attached to your wrists and ankles again and pulled firmly to fixtures on the floor about a metre apart. You are stretched out over the bench with no movement possible. Only your weighted balls swing between your legs. A wide belt across your back further anchors you to the bench. Finally a bit gag is forced into your mouth and buckled tightly at the back of your head. The only thing you can see is the floor in front of you and the metal tray under the bench to catch any fluids that might leak from you. You are immobile, gagged and without any way to avoid the inevitable abuse. You think it curious that they have left your arse unplugged, but realize it would not be empty for long.

The Masters seem pleased with their workmanship and the last you hear is the sound of them leaving the house, then the roar of the van engine as it makes off down the driveway. You are alone, chained and gagged in some remote house, somewhere in Germany. What have you let yourself in for, you wonder?

As the hours pass your jaws ache from the bit gag and you are bursting to piss. Eventually you can hold your piss no longer and let it spray into the tray. The PA ring ensures that it makes a mess everywhere. It is impossible to swallow your spit so you let it dribble around the bit gag and into the tray below. You know it is getting towards lunchtime because the house is heating up under the midday sun. You enjoy being chained up like this, and whilst you know the house is isolated, you realize you are at the mercy of anyone who calls in and decides to take advantage of your upturned and unprotected arse. This element of danger adds to your excitement and your erection adds to your discomfort.

Your prayers are answered when you hear the van pull up outside the house. Also you hear several motorbikes rev to a stop. The sound of heavy boots clumping around in the house and the smell of hot leather precedes the vision of booted, leather-clad legs standing around you. You count at least three pairs of boots, not including those of your three Masters. You recognize your Masters' boots from before; you had spent many hours cleaning them with your tongue and polish. Rough fingers poke into your arse and mouth.

'OK guys, easy now. He's not going anywhere,' says Master Ian. 'Let's eat first.'

The group disappears into the kitchen and you hear crockery and cutlery being moved around, chairs scraping on the floor and tins being opened. Master Peter returns with a protein drink for you and, after removing the gag, allows you to suck this up through a straw. You are grateful for the sustenance and drink every last drop. Instead of replacing the bit gag, he inserts the O-ring gag, once again buckling it tightly behind your head.

After lunch and a few beers the laughter is noticeably louder. The group sits around you and without any formalities Masters Mark and Peter take their positions at your head and arse. Master Mark releases the chains on your wrists and padlocks them behind your back, then with a short chain, lifts your wrists to your neck collar. This forces your head up and outwards. Without ceremony he thrusts his cock through the O-ring and mercilessly fucks you in the mouth. Master Peter needs only a condom and some lubricant before he is pounding away at your arse. You realize your arse has regained some of its tone, having not had a butt plug in it for the past six hours.

Other Masters crowd around to watch the action, offering comments on how to fuck, to the amusement of others. After an eternity, Masters Peter and Mark give their positions to two guests. They are noticeably rougher than your Masters. One grabs the back of your head, forcing you to take the entire length of his cock, whilst the other buries his cock in your arse up to the hilt. In a short time their sweat mingles with yours and they both blow their loads.

The third duo precedes their turn by whipping your arse with a cane until your buttocks are red. Each strike sends your balls swinging and waves of pain through your buttocks. You cry out through the gag but this does not diminish the power of their strokes. You are unable to move your arse but your head jerks up with every stroke, your bound wrists pulling painfully back on your neck collar. Master Ian pushes two, then three, then four fingers into your arse as the third guest fucks your face. The pain in your arse is nothing compared to the pain in your buttocks from the whipping, and by this time you are used to the feeling of hard cock against the back of your throat. Master Ian removes his hand and inserts a large butt plug, which he ties in with rope around your waist, then between your legs, encircling your cock and balls. The plug slips in easily and you are grateful for the rope because you feel the plug might otherwise slip out.

Once the pounding in your mouth has stopped, the Masters step back and help themselves to more beer. You hang limply over the bench with your battered and plugged arse raised up and your cuffed wrists pulling your head painfully backwards. The O-ring gag is removed and the dick gag reinserted and buckled in place. Try as your will you cannot ease the pain in your neck, other than by keeping your head bent backwards.

Eventually you are released from your flexed position on the bench, but you notice the chains still dangle from your ankles, and your wrists are still attached to the back of your neck. You are lifted up onto the bench so that your legs straddle it, and the butt plug is pushed further into your arse. The chains attached to your ankles are pulled sideways and are attached to fixtures on the floor. Chains are attached to the front and back of your collar and to the ends of the bench. You are firmly fixed to the bench, with the plug up your arse, the gag blocking your mouth and your hands cuffed and brought up to the back of your neck. Someone pulls your ball ring forward and anchors it to the bench, sending erotic messages to your cock, which is erect and straining forwards. The PA is grabbed, forced down to the bench and padlocked to the ball ring chain, causing spasms of pain in your cock throughout its whole length. You are stimulated at every point, cock, balls, arse and mouth. You groan into your gag, but cannot move. Every device causes your cock to strain against the padlocked PA, but you can do nothing.

'Rest easy boy. See you later,' someone says from behind you, as they all make their way out of the house and down the driveway, in a hale of gravel and exhaust.

You find that if you remain perfectly still, you are not in too much pain. If you move anything, your balls pull against the ring, the plug pumps into your arse and your wrists pull painfully downwards on your neck. Not least is the constant pressure your cock is under, anchored downwards as it is by the padlocked PA. So your time is spent trying not to move a muscle, which is OK for a while, until some ache causes you to involuntarily move, sending waves of pain through every part that is constricted or chained. There is no point is crying out; the gag prevents any effective noise, and anyway you are in the middle of nowhere, in a foreign country, and without any visible means of support. You suffer in painful, but erotic silence.

As the day turns to dusk you hear the van return. Within a few minutes your Masters take you from the bench and remove all your items of torture, except the metal shackles and the ball ring. They push you outside into the shower and you are grateful for its soothing coolness around your buttocks and arse, which are red from abuse. After drying yourself you are taken back inside the house and given more protein drink. While you are taking your drink your Masters discuss arrangements for the evening. They have booked one slave each from the slave register and have planned to enjoy them separately and together.

You are pointed to your leather clothes and, without prompting, pull on the leather pants, jacket and high boots. Everything fits perfectly and you realize that the Masters have gone to much trouble to have you looking good for the slave bookings. A hood and gag are tied tightly over your head, the metal neck collar still visible beneath. Your wrist cuffs are padlocked behind you and a chain attached to your collar. You are led outside and the chain leash wrapped around a tree. Compared to the abuse you had had during the day, this is truly a heavenly bondage.

You appreciate being able to see something of your place of incarceration and torture through the eyeholes in the hood. The house is small but well built and in the middle of the forest. A gravel driveway sweeps up to the house and immaculate gardens complete the effect. The appearance is that of discrete wealth and attention to detail. This fits in with the way Master Ian has arranged this trip, leaving nothing to chance, and taking every care that you, and Masters Mark and Peter, enjoy yourselves.

Day turns to night. Eventually the three Masters come out of the house and release you from the tree, but do not undo your wrists, which remain padlocked behind your back. You are ordered to sit in the back of the van with your back against the pole. Your elbows are drawn back behind the post by ropes, and this prevents you from sliding when the van turns corners. The Masters are dressed like you, in leather pants and jackets and high boots. Each has on a Master's cap. They check they have the keys to their respective booked slaves' padlocks.

It is Saturday evening and the roads around the leather quarter are packed. They manage to park two blocks away and, without any compromise to the original plan, untie your arms and pull you out of the van. Bystanders stare open mouthed at the four men in leather and boots, one of whom is hooded and shackled, with his wrists padlocked behind his back, being led by a chain down the street. You find this humiliating situation particularly stimulating and your cock starts to get a life all its own again.

The streets become progressively more and more populated by men in leather, some dragging bound slaves, others just standing around looking. In a short time you are at the slave corner, obvious by the six, leather clad and hooded men standing with their backs to poles with their wrists padlocked behind. These poles have been erected by the local leather club and prove a huge attraction, thereby increasing its business. You also notice one naked man hog tied and gagged, with his wrists and ankle drawn upwards to a cross bar on the pole. This is a Master undergoing punishment for mistreating a slave. From time to time someone will piss on him and he is wallowing in a puddle of piss and dirt.

After a few words with a man at the front door of the club, you are led to a pole and your padlocked wrists relocked behind the pole. The Masters then go around the other slaves, progressively trying their keys in their padlocks, until one key succeeds in releasing a slave, then another, then another. You watch your Masters lead their slaves away by chain leashes and then realize you are really on your own. You stand there in your leather and boots, hooded, gagged and padlocked to a pole in a public street. You are grateful for the hood, which hides your embarrassment. But as you look around you notice that no one thinks the situation is in any way unusual; it is just another night on the slave corner. Leather clad people mill around. The other slaves stand still and are not bothered when Masters try keys in their padlocks. Occasionally one fits and the slave is led away to some waiting car. Several Masters try to unlock your padlock but without success and from the furtive way they do this then walk quickly away, you know they are not registered Masters. Slaves are brought in and padlocked to the poles and others are taken away; the system seems to be an integral part of the leather / Master / slave community, and has the approval of all concerned. At one point a naked, gagged man is led out of the club and hog tied to another pole, and you know that yet another Master is being punished for transgressing the code of conduct. He seems resigned to his fate as the rope is hauled up over the cross beam and his back arched painfully. This is the only way to get back onto the Register of Masters; he has to suffer this pain and humiliation.

After an hour you feel a key turning in your padlock. Your wrists are quickly padlocked again behind your back and you feel strong hands push you to your knees on the sidewalk. A chain is attached to your collar and you are pulled to your feet. With instructions in German, that you do not understand, you are led away.

PART 11

As you struggle to walk through the streets, you reflect on your situation. You had voluntarily allowed yourself to be taken to a foreign country, tied up, fucked in the mouth and arse, abused and tortured, now collared, handcuffed, hooded and gagged, you are being led away by someone you do not know, to a fate you can only dream about. Are you anxious? Yes. Are you worried? No. Are you excited beyond anything you had ever dreamed about? Of course. The combination of inescapable bondage and the prospect of unpredictable sexual servitude has aroused you to the highest level of anticipation and excitement. Your erect cock, confined within its leather encasement, attests to this.

You detect that the leather crowd slowly gives way to the straight weekend, restaurant crowd as you venture further and further from the leather bars and the slave corner. Most people stop and stare at the leather clad, bound slave being marched through the streets, but you don't care. You are just happy to be led along by a member of the fraternity of Masters, whose aim is to provide service to slaves and Masters alike.

The Master has parked his car down a side alley, dark and damp, with treacherous cobblestones underfoot. The dark coloured Mercedes is a stark contrast to the van that Master Ian owned and used to transport you earlier in the evening. He opens the passenger door and guides you into the seat. A padlock secures your collar to the seat and he puts the seat belt on. You detect a faint odour of new leather in the car, unsure if it is coming from the car itself or his leather clothes, but it's an odour that always excites you.

The car speeds off but you have no idea where it is heading. The pin holes in the mask do not allow you see more than a small fraction of the view ahead and, being a foreign country to you, one street looks much like any other. You are aware that the town is giving way to countryside as first the streetlights, then the houses disappear. On and on, the car glides, effortlessly down empty roads edged by tall grass and ghostly trees. You notice on the car clock that two hours pass and you begin to wonder if something is wrong. The Master says nothing, his gaze fixed on the darkness ahead and your occasional grunt into the gag results in nothing. Where can you be going, you wonder?

As three hours approaches the car pulls into a sweeping gravel driveway and a large, ramshackle house looms into view. At the front of the house a large black car glistens in the moist night air. A uniformed driver stands beside the car and jumps to attention as the Mercedes approaches. The Master shouts out to the uniformed driver, who rushes to the passenger door, opens it and releases you from the seat. Still cuffed, hooded and gagged, you struggle out of the car and are then marched towards a side door, some distance from the main door of the house.

The uniformed driver seems confident as he pushes and guides you down stairs and steadies you against a cement post, while he padlocks your collar to a short chain on the post. The chain permits neither movement up, down nor to the sides, but retains you upright, with head firmly pointing forwards. The driver leaves you and walks back to the house. He walks with the confident stride of someone who has done this many times before.

Once again you resign yourself to a period of inescapable bondage, chained by your metal neck collar to a post, hooded and gagged, encased in leather and at the mercy of whomever passes by. The dark, damp, subterranean room in which you are locked appears isolated from the world; no sound or light reaches you and you barely make out the slime on the walls. You drift off to sleep but only for a few seconds, because you startle awake when the pressure from your fixed neck collar obstructs your breathing. Your arms and shoulders are beginning to ache from the cuffs and you desperately want to piss.

It seems hours before the Master descends the stairs. He flicks on a light, just a bare globe above your head, which demonstrates that he is not alone. Behind him stand the driver and two Middle Eastern looking men, whose dress is like something out of Lawrence of Arabia. They mutter between themselves then address the Master.

'We need to see him naked,' the taller one says.

'Certainly,' say the Master.

With a gesture of his head, Master indicates to the driver to release you.

He unlocks your neck and the padlock around your wrist cuffs. The hood is removed, as is all your leather clothing and boots. You stand there, shivering, in just your metal neck collar, wrist and ankle cuffs. You dare not look the others in the eye, for your training is now ingrained. With a riding crop, the taller Arab lifts your chin but you continue to look at the floor. He circles you and prods you all over. He pushes you to bend forwards and, with a rubber-gloved hand, inserts two, three, four fingers into your arse. He is not gentle, but you withstand the urge to cry out, only the tears in your eyes reveal the pain. He tweaks your ringed nipples, which causes them to become erect.

'Nice job,' say the Arab. 'We will take him as he is. He seems well trained and is in good shape. We can make preparations in the morning.'

They depart, leaving only the driver, who orders you to go to the corner and piss in the bucket. He then points you to a bowl on the floor containing gruel; you suck up the mixture in the bowl. You are relieved to empty your bladder and the mixture tastes curiously sweet, not like the protein mixture you had before. You've no idea what the mixture is, but gulp the lot as you are so hungry. The drive tells you to dress in the leathers and boots, then padlocks your wrists behind you again. He reattaches the short chain to your neck, but relocates it to an eyebolt on the post at sitting height. Without further discussion, he leaves. The door remains ajar an inch, so that only moonlight illuminates the dreary, damp cellar. Within a short time, you feel drowsy, then it twigs that the mixture must have contained a sedative. You fall asleep, sitting on the cement floor and propped against the pillar.

Sleep comes and goes. If you sleep bolt upright, everything is OK. If you sway to one side you startle awake as the pressure from your collar obstructs either your breathing or the blood flow to your head. Your hands remain uncomfortably cuffed behind you and you constantly need to prevent yourself from pressing them into the pillar.

The night passes interminably slowly and after what seems a lifetime, light starts to appear at the chink in the doorframe. It's still another hour before shuffling sounds are heard overhead, the door opens and the driver descends the stairs. He offers no greeting, just dumps a dog bowl of food on the floor, releases your neck then disappears into the gloom behind you.

You shuffle to your knees and gulp the food, doggy style. It tastes like porridge with lots of sugar, but it fills a deep gnawing in your stomach and you are secretly grateful for it. The driver reappears and refills your bowl, with the curt instruction, 'Eat.' You keenly suck up the second dish, trying not to slurp food on your leathers or around your face.

As you lick the bowl clean, the driver releases your wrists then tells you to take off all your clothes. Standing there naked again, you wonder what can be next in this curious journey. You are particularly interested in the Arabs, who promise some excitement today. The driver grabs your neck and leads to an adjacent room, which is a bathroom, of sorts. A filthy toilet stands next to an equally filthy hand basin. A tap coming out of the wall at head level is an excuse for a shower and a central drain hole is encrusted with dried muck. The driver points you towards a bar of soap, a toothbrush and toothpaste, a razor and soap and a towel. You get the point. The driver leaves and you start your ablutions.

It's not easy to shave and shower with heavy iron manacles, but you are grateful for the opportunity to clean the crap out of your mouth and from your body. You try to shit but nothing comes out. You feel almost human again, but one glance at your image in the cracked mirror reveals a slave wearing manacles and an iron collar, and this leaves you in no doubt as to your real persona.

As you stand there drinking in your image, an image you've been wishing for, for a long time, the driver reappears and motions you to bend forwards. He eases a moderate sized butt plug into your arse and ties it in place with rope. He orders you to dress again in the leathers and boots. You relish at the thought of, once again, being encased in leather and boots. Whatever lies at the end of this journey will inevitably mean partial, if not complete, nakedness, and lots of heavenly discomfort, humiliation and pain.

Instead of padlocking your wrists again, the drive urges you up the stairs and towards the main door of the house. In the daylight you appreciate the opulent, yet faded decadence of the property, with its gables and creeping ivy, manicured flower beds gone to seed and the landscaped garden, stretching to the horizon, and much in need of attention. But the house appears well used, with worn tracks in the driveway. Where once stood the two cars, is now a van, similar to Master Ian's, black in colour and highly polished. This was no utility van, with its tinted windows, mag wheels and discrete motifs on the doors. The number plate told the whole story, S4M 1.

PART 12

Inside the front door a huge chandelier illuminates a vast entry hall, oak panelled and lined with Egyptian relics. A faint smell of incense lingers in the air. The house does not reflect the unkempt gardens, being spotlessly clean, with gleaming brassware and sparkling mirrors. The driver hastily pushes you into a small side room, which is devoid of any of the opulence of the hallway, just a few chairs and a large box in the middle. A smaller box to one side is open and reveals chains and rope and numerous padlocks. This must be the playroom, you thought. How wrong you were.

The driver pushes you to an area in the middle of a circle of chairs. You automatically assume the slave's position, keeling, with your head bowed and hands behind your back. The driver leaves. There is little point in attempting an escape because you have no idea where you are and anyway, you want to be here. The anticipation is building, when the entire crowd, Arabs, Master and driver, enters the room and sits on the chairs around you. The driver orders you to lie down on your back on the floor. The Master opens your fly and extracts your cock, now semi rigid but rapidly deflating in the cool morning air. The driver produces a catheter and you prepare for the discomfort of being catheterised again. The Master dons sterile gloves, washes your dick and squirts the gel down your piss hole before inserting the catheter. You jump at the temporary pain as the catheter enters your bladder and then relax as the piss is released. The retaining balloon is inflated and the end of the catheter attached to a plastic bag, which is attached to your thigh.

The driver produces duct tape and proceeds to wrap your head, from top to neck, leaving only a hole for your nostrils. Although your mouth is empty, there is no chance to make any sound as your lips are firmly taped closed. Several layers of tape ensure your head appears as a smooth, shinny, black ball. Two well-lubricated tubes are pushed into your nostrils and taped in place, and the security of your breathing is assured.

A door to the larger box is opened and you are pushed inside and onto a wooden bench built into the floor of the box. There is barely room for you to straighten your back when the driver locks your collar to the back wall of the box. Your wrists are locked to eyebolts at the sides and your ankles are similarly locked together and to the floor. Rope binds your legs tightly together and further rope binds your arms and torso to the back of the box. You are absolutely fixed in place with no movement possible in any direction. Your arse is plugged, so nothing is going to leak out of there, and your piss is taken care of by the catheter. You wonder how long this will be for. And what's with the box anyway?

You start to panic when you hear the door of the box being closed, then screwed down with an electric drill. As it happens, there are air holes around the box and handles and arrows indicate which way is top. You start to realise this is going to be no ordinary journey.

Masters Ian, Peter and Mark were expecting you back within a day of your being taken at slave corner, and in one piece. It's about now you should be returned to your owners and soon they will start retrieval proceedings, as stated in the regulations for this arrangement. The National Registers of Masters and Slaves have strict protocols in place for the non-return or abuse of slaves. When a Master fails to return a slave on time, the punishment is a heavy fine for periods under one day. Thereafter he suffers the same fate as those who abuse or injure slaves, stript naked, hog tied to a post at slave corner and left there for others to use as a toilet. When extensive searches for lost slaves are needed, the Master is 'captured' and forced to the status of a slave himself, for periods determined by a committee of Masters and slaves. The usual period is three months, during which time the Master, now reduced to the level of a slave's slave, is kept in chains at a rural farm, forced to work during the day in shackles, abused at night by slaves and left gagged and shackled to a drain at all other times. He pisses and shits into the drain and is hosed off with cold water in the mornings, prior to the days work. Masters subjected to this punishment rarely offend again. You are confident that Master Ian will commence proceedings for your rescue as soon as the agreed return time passes.

The box, in which you are now effectively a prisoner, is lifted up and carried to the back of the van outside. You are firmly fixed inside the box but suffer every jar and bump as it is manoeuvred into the back of the van. After more bumping around in the back of the van and the sound of doors closing, the van takes off down the dirt road, then speeds along the highway. Every bump sends shock waves up your arse, as the butt plug is hammered further in. There is no way you can relieve the pressure.

After about ten minutes the van slows and finally comes to a halt. The smell of aviation gas gives you a hint that you are at an airport, somewhere. The van doors open and after more pushing and pulling, the box is hoisted onto a forklift and eased into the back of a small plane, you presume. The rich smell of leather and tropical spices suggests this is no economy class passenger plane. Further shuffling sounds and voices in Arabic do not encourage you that you will see your owners soon, if ever again, but you can do nothing. You are firmly bound, gagged, plugged and catheterised and have no control over your body, what will happen to it or where you are going.

The engines start and, with incredible acceleration, you leap down the runway and are soon airborne. You are sure this is a jet; it is smooth, fast and quiet, unlike your economy trip to Germany, plugged, in the back of a commercial plane last week. All you can hear is the muffled sounds of voices, the chinking of glasses and the occasional door closing. After an hour or so, the voices die down and give way to a soft hum from the engines. It seems that everyone has gone to sleep but that luxury evades you as your mind concentrates on your various aches and pains. The butt plug is comfortable, providing you do not move an inch. The catheter in your dick causes a constant sting. Your tightly bound head is an irritation but you can do nothing about it. Occasionally you drift into a twilight state, but your bonds keep you from actually falling asleep.

You are aroused when the plane touches down and you startle when you realise your situation, tied up in a box, heading towards god knows where. Eventually your box is lifted out of the plane and onto the back of a truck, while the accompanying Arab ensemble heads for a waiting Mercedes. The road seems smooth but it's as hot as hell and you start to sweat profusely inside your leathered prison.

Mercifully, the journey is short and the truck stops in an underground garage, somewhere. The box is hoisted from the back of the truck and placed on the ground. The front of the box is opened and the rush of cool air is a huge relief. Your padlocks and bonds are removed and you are manhandled out of the box and dumped on the floor, still dressed in leathers and boots and with your head tightly taped. Arms hold you firmly to the ground while the catheter is removed. Someone strips you of your boots and leathers and your wrists are padlocked behind your back again. A short but heavy chain is padlocked between your metal ankle cuffs, not that you are thinking of going anywhere. You are turned face down while someone urges the butt plug from your arse. It slides out easily, followed by gas, but no fluid. You are lifted onto a chair. You feel someone start to remove the tape around your head by sliding scissors down the side of your head and cutting through the tape, then peeling it off in one mess of tape and sweat. You think to keep your eyes closed, as the sudden burst of light is sure to be painful.

As the final strip of tape is torn from your head, you attempt to open your eyes.

'You can open your eyes and look at us,' a rich, cultured voice says.

You coax our eyes open and drink in the surrounds. You are in an underground garage but the only cars there, other than the truck you came in, are two Rolls Royces and a Mercedes. The two Arabs you saw in Germany sit before you on an ornate sofa and several other Arabs stand behind them. At the feet of the Arabs are two slaves, shackled hand and foot and collared with a metal band, which appears welded in place. Chains from the metal collars are held by the Arabs on the sofa. The slaves are sun tanned and have the appearance of men who work out in the gym all day. Their heads are shaved. The slaves have nose rings of heavy stainless steel, which enhance their absolute captivity.

'You are in Arabia, you don't need to know exactly where,' the shorter Arab says.

'We bought you from the Master in Germany. We rely on him to procure quality slaves for us, so we hope you will not disappoint us. You are now our property. We, and other dignitaries, including the Sultan, need slaves to run our properties, work on the land and to service us whenever we demand. We are the procurers and keepers of slaves in this land, which stretches far as the eye can see. Our subjects know we are ruthless and should you escape, they will not hesitate to apprehend you and return you to us, for which they will receive a handsome reward. We do not need guards when our subjects are so faithful.'

Your mind was spinning. How can this have happened? You were assured of security when you were taken to the slave corner. Had your European Masters double-crossed you? You felt sure the German Master had doublecrossed them, and sincerely hope he will live to pay the price. You cannot believe, after all you have gone through with Masters Mark, Peter and Ian, that they will have let you down like this, and allow you to be sold into slavery in some foreign country.

'Sir, please, what about my Masters in Europe. They are expecting me back,' you plea.

Whack! A whip lashes your chest. You scream with pain as a thin line of blood forms where the whip struck.

'Don't speak slave. Your opinion is of no concern to us. You belong to us now.'

Your tear-filled eyes glance at the slaves on the floor, who plead with you with their eyes for you to remain silent.

'Insert the ring,' the taller Arab commands.

Several Arabs grab your head and steady it while another pulls down on your nose and rams a wide needle through the septum. The pain is transient but blood spurts onto your chest. A wide metal ring is forced into the hole made by the needle and the ends are forced together with heavy pliers and

spot welded shut. The bleeding soon stops but the heavy ring pulls down on
your nose and causes tears to well up in your eyes. Someone washes your
face and applies cream around the ring, twisting it round to ensure that all
parts are covered.

You realise that things are serious now. Will you ever see your European
Masters again? Will you survive this enforced slavery? And where the hell
are you?

'Take him away.'

The two slaves shuffle to their feet and, led by two Arab keepers, help you
to your feet. You all shuffle off, each step being constrained by your recent
confinement and the short chain between your ankles. The slaves help you
as best they can but their hands are manacled and all they can do is hold your
cuffed arms. The Arabs lead the way through carpeted rooms and exotically
tiled corridors. Gold leaf drips from ornate fittings and fixtures. Through
the windows you see lush gardens, fountains and tropical birds, giving way
to a relentless ocean of desert sand in the distance. A heavy wooden door
leads to steep stairs, which you descend with help of the slaves. In the
basement a long stone corridor leads to a series of cells, each with a heavy
iron door and a grill at eye level. One of the Arabs opens a door and slaves
ease you into the dimly lit cell, then follow you, as though they know what
to do.

As the door slams and is locked, you notice the two slaves have taken the
initiative and filled a cracked glass with water for you. You gulp down the
water in one go and they refill the glass, before sitting on a pile of straw.

You have no idea who these slaves are, but they appear Caucasian, albeit
sunburned. A few sentences confirm that they are German, but speak
excellent English. Their stories of kidnap and transportation mirror yours,
and it seems they have been in Arabia for almost a year. You had heard
a story of men missing from a gay beach resort last year, but paid little
attention to it. It seems the guys were picked up in a bar at the resort, then
cuffed, hooded and gagged, led to a car and driven to the same house in the
country where you were 'processed'.

They had given up hope of escape and were convinced they would die in Arabia. They worked during the day in the fields and castle. At nights they were rented out to castle staff or members of the community, for sex. The only conditions imposed on the renters were that they must not mark or damage the slaves. Those who disobeyed were subject to a period of slavery themselves. Almost every night then, the slaves were restrained, flogged and fucked. Sometimes they were forced to service women; sometimes they were just strung up. Rarely a weekend would go by without the slaves being gagged, oiled and strung between posts in the middle of a dinner party, to be later taken down and publicly fucked, or chained to a post in the yard as garden furniture. If a renter complained that their arses were too tight they would be forced to spend the night with a dildo shoved up their arses, tied in with leather thongs. The renter would then get a free nights use of the slave.

At any time the chief Arabs would take them and abuse them, in the cell, in the house or in the garden. It seemed there were other slaves at the castle, Blacks from Africa and Asians from Thailand. It was a thriving business and the slaves observed that renters came from all parts of Arabia to make use of the facility. The Sultan, too, kept a stable of slaves and other wealthy people in the town kept smaller, working stables of slaves.

If a slave got sick, they would be transported back to their home country, at night, and dumped, naked, by the roadside, to find their own way home. Usually the police would arrest them, but write them off as some crazy person, with a weird story about being kept as a slave in a foreign country.

Completely exhausted, you slump onto the straw, wrists still cuffed behind your back. The pain in your nose has reduced to a dull ache and only when you turn your head are you reminded of the heavy metal ring through it. The two slaves, grateful for your company, snuggle up to you as best they can in their own shackles, and together you fall asleep.

PART 13

You sleep long and deep. Throughout the night you wonder what your European Masters are doing. Surely they are making moves to find you and return you to their care.

In Germany, all is not well. Maters Ian, Mark and Peter are angry beyond words when the Master fails to return you to the slave corner the following day. They wait for half a day in the bar. The slaves they returned are taken away by their owners but there is no sign of you. That afternoon they alert the keepers of the Register of Masters, to find out that the Master who took you was an impostor, having stolen the padlock key from a friend, who was to have taken you that evening.

The following morning they track down the friend, the real Master. He is horrified to learn that his friend had stolen his key; he thought he had just mislaid it. He is even more shocked to hear of the non-return of the slave; such offences must not go unpunished, he says. He eagerly supplies the address of the impostor and your Masters make all haste to drive to this house in the country.

On arrival, the impostor is alone and denies all knowledge of you, of course, but the presence of duct tape and rope suggests he knows more than he is letting on. As they are being ushered out of the house, Master Ian notices his padlock, the one that attached you to the post at slave corner, lying on the table. He whirls round on the impostor and grabs him by the neck.

'You bastard, he was here, I know it. Where is he?' he screams.

'I don't know what you are talking about,' the impostor gasps.

'OK, then where did you get this padlock of mine?' Master Ian challenges.

'Well, I, found it in the street,' came the pathetic excuse.

'Why would someone who owns a Mercedes and a country mansion pick up a padlock in the street? You fucking liar.' Master Ian tightens his grip on the impostor's neck as Masters Peter and Mark rush to grab rope from the other room.

Struggle as he did, the impostor could not break from the Master Ian's strangling grip on his neck. The other Masters return and quickly tie the impostor's hands behind his back and around his chest. Master Ian releases his grip and secures a tight noose around the impostor's neck, yanking at the rope so that the impostor falls to the ground. His ankles are quickly tied and brought up to his wrists in a painful hog tie. Further rope is wrapped around his thighs to reinforce the hog tie, and around his mouth to act as a partial, but painful, gag.

A rope is slung to a beam on the ceiling and around the impostors hog tie, so that his back is painfully arched and his head pulled back. Your three Masters slowly relax and wonder where to go from here.

The impostor is not going anywhere, so they retire to the kitchen and help themselves to some food and wine while they contemplate their next move. A quick look around the house reveals the full extent of the situation. In the basement, hooks on the walls and posts, left over bits of rope and the smell of piss prove the recent presence of people held against their will. In the house, a chest full of rope, handcuffs, shackles and duct tape confirm an extensive operation.

They return to the hogtied, impostor and make themselves comfortable on chairs around.

'OK, it's like this you fucker. Either you tell us where our slave is or we burn your house down. Either way, you will be subject to the law of the Register of Masters, which means a heavy fine and at least three months servitude as a slave. And we will make sure you get sent only to the cruellest of Masters. We could also turn you over to the police, who we are sure, will relish the thought of prosecuting a slave trader. And anyway, we are sure your business partners would like to know of your extra curricula activities, and how you've come to afford this mansion.'

Master Peter leans forwards and removes the rope gag from the impostor, at the same time he hitches up the rope between the hogtie and ceiling beam another notch, causing the impostor to groan with pain.

'Please, please. They forced me to do this. The Arabs said they would foreclose on the company if I did not help them get slaves. I could not let the company disintegrate. And now I've got in so deep I can't get out of it. If we loose the company, hundreds will be out of work and all our livelihoods will fall apart.' The impostor struggles to spit out sentences as his head is pulled back and breathing becomes difficult.

'The Arabs promised they would look after the slaves I sent them, but I only hear from them when they want replacements. Last month one of their slaves fell sick and was returned to Europe, so I had to find one in a hurry. I am sorry it had to be your personal slave; I usually get them from the street, but none were to be found last week and my friend was to pick up your slave, until I stole his key.'

'Yeah, yeah, but where is he,' spat Master Ian, his patience running short.

'Arabia,' the impostor replied. 'I don't know exactly where but I have documents that will let you track down his exact location.'

The three Masters looked at each other, wondering whether to believe the impostor. With a nod they release the bonds from the hogtied impostor but retie his hands behind his back and tighten the noose around his neck. Master Peter pulls him to his feet by pulling on the noose. Gasping, the impostor struggles to stand, at the same time Master Peter hitches up his bound wrists to the back of his neck by tying the noose around them. This means that any struggle of the wrists causes further tightening of the noose around his neck.

'OK shithead, where's the information?' asks Master Ian.

The impostor leads the way to an adjacent room and goes to a filing cabinet.

'Third drawer down, file marked 'International Finance Corp', towards the back of the drawer,' gasps the impostor, who is struggling to keep his neck back in order to breathe.

Master Ian grabs at the drawer and finds the file. Addresses from various letters and invoices suggest an address in Zurich and another in central Saudi Arabia. Master Mark searches for an atlas and locates this remote, desert town. Then, using the impostor's computer, searches more accurately for the place on Google Earth.

'Fuck me, this place is in the middle of nowhere,' says Master Mark. 'How are we going to get him out of there? Just an airstrip 10 Km away, no roads, no nothing.'

'Let me figure that out. Don't worry, I've got friends in the army who would love the job, to rescue a white hostage from this bunch,' offers Master Ian, who seems to have contacts far and wide.

They bundle up the papers and their new prisoner and head for home. In the city they take the now contrite prisoner to the president of the Register of Masters, who locks him up in their basement cells, to await the next hearing for judgement. He promises the three Masters that justice will be done. They had never had a case of slave trading and he was sure they committee would take a very dim view and enforce the severest of punishments.

Armed with the information and the secure knowledge that the impostor will not be making any further attempts to kidnap and export slaves, they return to Master Ian's house to contemplate their next move.

'This is going to have to be completely informal,' offers Master Ian. 'and secret. I know my army friends have connections with the government, which will 100% support our moves, but they can't be seen to be dabbling in the rescue of slaves. My friends are SAS trained and have conducted similar convert operations in Africa and South America in the past, with great success. Let me talk to them this evening. It helps that two of them are on the Register of Masters and another two are registered slaves, so we will have their full cooperation. Their leader, Hans, has recently confessed his desire to be a slave too, although he remains my strongest team leader. In the meantime I suggest you both go back to England and prepare to receive your slave.'

Much as Masters Peter and Mark wanted to be more active in the rescue, they did not speak German, they had no SAS training and agreed they would only be in the way. Reluctantly they resolve to pack up and return to England.

PART 14

You sleep soundly, although shackled with your hands behind your back. Your fellow slaves nestle against you during the night and provide some of the comfort and warmth that has been lacking in your life of late. Even though you are helpless to protect yourself, neither slave molests you, rather they hug and caress you, sooth your aches and pains and allay your anxieties. Little did you know what was in store for you.

As the burning desert sun crept into the skylight of your cell, the door flies open and the Arab keepers storm in and grab you by your chains, dragging you out of the cell. They remove the padlocks to your wrists and the chains around your ankles, then bundle you under a cold tap. You are grateful for the opportunity to wash since you have been stewing all night in dried sweat and dirt. The other slaves smelt clean and you were embarrassed by your pungent odour. You vigorously scrub away the crud, using the soap and harsh brush, which the keepers threw on the floor. Still wet and dripping, the keepers lead you to a side room, more of a barn, where you see three other slaves chained in the stalls. All are naked apart from metal collars, which keep them firmly chained to the wall. They all seem disinterested in the new recruit and barely lift an eyelid when you are dragged into their stable.

The keeper thrusts a bowl of porridge at you and you tip it down your throat as fast as you can. Another bowl and some dried bread follow and you bolt it down. A bucket is the only water supply and a cup on a chain enables you to wash the whole lot down.

Without waiting the keepers thrust you over a bench and, whilst one holds your head down, the other opens your legs and seeks out your arse. Without ceremony he greases your arse and eases in a butt plug with a difference. It's a large butt plug and you struggle to accommodate it but eventually your arse squeezes around its narrow neck. At the end of the plug are horsehairs, so the impression is of you having a tail. You had worn a dog tail before and are excited at this animalisation and humiliation. The keeper straps the tail in by passing straps around your waist and between your legs. It is impossible to push the tail out.

The keepers stand you upright and padlock your wrists behind your back again, then use rope to bring you arms further together behind your back, so that your elbows almost touch. A tight fitting leather hood is laced on your head and a bit gag inserted and tied behind your head. Chains pass from the gag and your metal collar to the wall of the stable. A harness is strapped to your chest and waist to which leather reins are attached. A metal ball weight is locked around the top of your balls and connected to the tail by a short chain, so that your now erect cock strains forwards. High heeled, high leg boots are laced on your legs. You have become a human pony.

The keepers hold the chains and reins and whip you into running around the stable. You quickly get the hang of lifting your feet high, so as not to trip. They pull your bit gag to the right and left and you learn to turn accordingly. When they pull both chains together you know to stop. Next they attach a riding buggy and sit in it. It's hard work pulling them around the stable with its rough floor but you imagine it to be easier on the paved road. Your tail and balls swing in the wind as you trot around the stable.

In quick succession the other three stable slaves are similarly geared up, each with a tail and the full range of pony gear. They stand still while they are kitted out and you know they are used to this routine. Each human pony is attached to poles at the side, so they pull the buggy as a single unit. The keepers whip the team into action, out of the stable and along the road to the front of the castle. No one says anything; what is there to say anyway.

You are a human pony, whose job is to haul people around. No discussion needed.

The pony team waits while the keepers disappear into the castle. As the sun rises, the doors open and one of the chief Arabs and a small boy come out and quietly sit in the buggy. The whip cracks across your shoulders and the team lurches into action, pulling the buggy out of the driveway and along the road.

A slow trot is all that is possible, despite repeated flogging. You pass people walking by the roadside, but they hardly give you a glance. Towards the town you see other human ponies pulling buggies and soon realise that this is the dominant form of transport in the area. The Arab guides you towards a school, at which the child gets out. Without a break he guides the team towards an office building in the middle of town. The rails outside the building are specifically designed for human ponies and a row of water bottles with plastic tubes at their neck enable the ponies to drink, whilst waiting for their charges. The Arab ties the buggy to the rail and leaves his ponies by the roadside.

You each drink the water, which is automatically refilled. Even though the sun is high, you drink excess water and soon need to piss. Embarrassed and not knowing what to do you glance at the next pony, which indicates to the road, and he relieves himself as he stands. Your erect cock and PA ring ensure your piss splashes everywhere, and you spread your legs wide to avoid getting piss on your boots

People pass by without glancing at the human pony team in the road. There are many other such teams, composed of black, white, brown and Asian human ponies. There must be a vigorous international slave trade to keep all these pony teams stocked. How has all this happened without your knowledge, you wonder?

Towards noon, the Arab returns to his buggy and whips you all back to the castle. Back in the stable the keepers take all the pony gear off and the tails out. There is a rush for the bucket toilets as the slaves have been plugged all morning and have not had the opportunity to shit. You follow but keep your distance until they are finished. How long, you wonder, will it be before you are similarly disinhibited and piss and shit in public like the rest of them?

The keepers bring more porridge, bread and water, which seem to be the staple diet. Wearing only your metal collar, nose ring, cuffs and ankle cuffs, you woof down the food and water, without a thought for table manners or etiquette. There is no table, so why worry. You are all permitted a ten minute rest before the chain shackles are locked back in place and further chains and locked between the metal neck collars, so you are all chained together. With considerable clanking of chains you are herded out of the barn and into the fields to one side of the castle.

As you approach the fields you notice other teams already working the ground. They are all chained together and working in unison, digging, hoeing, planting, and gathering fruit and vegetables. There is no mechanisation, just shovels, digging sticks and baskets, into which fruit and vegetables are placed. Efficiency depends on synchronised manual labour and the team quickly learns to work together to avoid the whips of the keepers. With wrists and ankles chained, you find it difficult to work the ground efficiently and when another slave stumbles, the whole team is dragged down and feels the whips of the keepers.

Every hour you are permitted a five-minute break, during which time the keepers offer water. The sweat pours from your skin so you know to drink deeply to avoid dehydration. You had noticed how fit all the slaves looked, now you know how they manage that; non-stop work in the outdoors.

The drudgery of the work is mind numbing; lean, dig, straighten, stoop, pick, basket. Hour after hour. The fine sandy soil oozes between your toes and gets between your manacles and skin, to mix with sweat and cause chaffing. All slaves have abrasions around their manacles.

Towards mid afternoon a whistle sounds and the keepers shout at their slaves, which, you presume, is an order of some kind. You just follow what other slaves are doing and form a line for the walk back to the stables. On the way back, a large trough is for washing the tools and another line of slaves stores them neatly in a shed.

Back at the stable, the slaves line up beneath a beam. The chain connecting your necks is removed and your wrist manacles are padlocked to the beam above your head. All the slaves seem used to this ritual and hang their heads in submission for whatever will happen. One keeper holds a large bore hose and proceeds to hose down the slaves. The water is cold and refreshing but is blasted against the slaves' skin so they have difficulty remaining upright. If you slip you hang by your wrist manacles. The cold water penetrates every orifice. You notice the mud stained water draining away from the stable.

After hosing down, slaves are left chained up to dry. There is no soap, no towels, no luxury of any kind, but somehow this does not bother you. You have coped well so far with your enforced slavery and although you continually think of your European Masters, you believe you can survive this experience. You glance at the other slaves hanging there, drying in the cool, dry air. They seem bound by a routine, resigned to their fate and many do not appear unduly unhappy.

After an hour or so, you are released from the beam and offered another bowl of porridge, only this time with meat scraps and vegetables. The food is quickly consumed and no one leaves a morsel. Slaves, still manacled, lounge on the straw. When the keepers leave the stable, conversation starts, but is muted, and in several different languages. You detect European tongues and the guttural tones of Arabic languages. Amidst the mumblings an American voice attracts your attention. You track the voice down to a tall, blond man in his early adulthood, just behind you.

'What's going on? What is going to happen?' you dare to ask him.

'They'll leave us alone till evening then they will come in and pick a couple of us for sex or for auction. You don't have any choice in who they pick. They will just grab your shackles and march you out. If you are lucky you will be chosen by one the educated household staff. But if you are being rented out to someone from outside, you will have a hard time of it.'

'How long have you been here?' you venture to ask.

'I was kidnapped from a camping site in France about six months ago, just as I was starting a year trip around Europe. No one knows I am missing as I told everyone I may be out of contact for a year. They shipped me here in a coffin, but I was drugged and do not remember most of the journey, only the butt plug and catheter, which hurt like hell. I thought I had died, until they opened the coffin and brought me here.

I've been a slave before, when I was in college in US, but only for a weekend. I like being restrained and forced to do sex with guys, but I also like getting back to my normal life again. This is merciless; endless work and sexual servitude. Man, before I came here I struggled to take a cock up the arse. Now they stick huge dildos up there and I can even take a small fist. Of course, I am always heavily restrained and gagged and often drugged up. When people rent you out they want their money's worth and really lay into you. Those who are getting you for free, some sort of barter arrangement, seem to take their time and treat you more gently. But fuck, I wanna go home.'

'Have you tried to escape?' you ask.

'Are you fucking crazy! There's nowhere to escape to and if they catch you, which they always do, they hang you up in the court yard and flog you within an inch of your life, then chain you up in the dungeon for weeks on end. It's the fucking pits, I am told. Nothing but bread and water to live on. Guys come out deathly white, skinny and hardly able to walk. Don't even think about it,' he warns.

A dark cloud passes over your mind. Will you never see your European Masters again? Will they try and reach you, here in the middle of the desert? Maybe they will just wash their hands of you and find another slave. You feel tears welling up in your eyes, and avert your gaze, so as not to be seen. You have no idea what other slaves are saying but a black slave close by, seeing your tears, stretches out his manacled hand to touch you gently on the cheek. You struggle to smile back. This brief moment of tenderness calms your troubled mind and you begin to think that you might survive.

Within an hour, the keepers are back. Two keepers pull a white slave from the group and one keeper indicates with his crooked finger for you to get up and follow him. You struggle to your feet. The American, Dale, is also selected and together you stand and move forwards. You notice that only white slaves are chosen and this, apparently, is the practice, to use mainly white slaves for rental and sex.

The keepers attach chains to your neck collars and pull you after them and towards a waiting group of Arabs. Your naked humiliation reveals itself as your cock stiffens. The slaves form a line whilst the Arabs sit around you on the floor. One slave steps forward and bidding starts. You have no idea what is being said, but it is apparent that biding is fast and furious. Eventually one Arab stands, claps his hands and steps forward to claim the slave. He drags him out of the room, to a fate only he will ever know. The arrangement is that any rented slave is returned, unharmed, in the morning and if this fails to happen, much like the slave arrangement in Germany, the bidder finds himself severely punished, although here, this takes the form of a public flogging in the town square, rather than service as a slave.

The American stands forward, and clearly he knows the protocol. He keeps his head bowed whilst the bidding takes place. He is a popular slave, tall, white and handsome. The Arabs argue amongst themselves and eventually a swarthy Arab, with immaculate robes, stands to claim him. Dale is forced to a kneeling position, while the Arab stuffs a gag into his mouth then uses duct tape to fix it in place. The tape is wrapped round and around his head so that only his eyes and nose are free. You notice tears well up in Dale's eyes as he is dragged from the room.

Your turn comes and you stand conspicuously in the middle of the remaining crowd. Whilst you may have dreamed of this situation for a long time, manacled hand and foot, collared and chained, ready to be sold as a slave at auction, you had always viewed this in a situation where the players would be known to you, or at least there was some Westernised normality to the affair. But here you are in a foreign country, just a piece of slave meat, about to be rented out to god-knows-who and to suffer a fate that is probably unimaginable back in Europe.

Curiously, the room becomes quiet. The jabbering Arabs fall silent when a door on the far wall opens and an imposing figure in a decorated robe enters. A retinue of impressively dressed Arabs and two slaves in harnesses and metal collars follows him. A nearby keeper mutters under his breath, but you hear the word 'Sultan' mentioned. The crowd parts as he moves forwards, directly towards you. You keep your eyes cast down and when he is directly in front, you notice his gold slippers and the immaculate gold-trimmed hem of his robe.

From his escorting party, two Arabs step forward and force you to your knees. A large pecker gag is buckled, then locked, into your mouth. Your elbows are pulled back and a rod thrust behind them, pulling your manacled hands up in front of you. The chain on your collar is pulled so that you stand up, and in immaculate English, the Sultan says,

'You come highly recommended and I have chosen you for a trial as my personal sex slave. If I am satisfied, you will be treated well. You will be returned to this slave facility and work alongside the other slaves for five days a week and for the others, you will be my personal slave. You will service me whenever and wherever I say. You will come to no harm, unless you disobey or try to escape.'

There was no pause for reflection. His two slaves step forward and drag you along at the rear of the party as they leave the room. Your manacled ankles clang along the tiled corridor and you shuffle quickly to keep up with the rest of the group. You are led to a waiting buggy, where your collar and the rod behind your back are attached to a central, vertical pole. The Sultan sits at the front of the buggy. The four human ponies at the front of the buggy lean forwards and slowly the buggy sets off down the road, followed by other buggies with the retinue, and the two slaves, who run immediately behind the Sultan's buggy.

The road is smooth, but nevertheless, the collar bites into your neck with each lurch and turn. The Sultan whips the ponies as the road steepens. Sweat drips from the ponies as they gasp and heave their load up the hill to an impressive looking palace at the top.

Manicured lawns and gardens surround the palace and guards open carved wooden gates as you approach. Inside the gate, palm trees and fountains create a cooling ambience, in contrast to the blistering nothingness of the desert outside.

The buggy draws up to the main door of the palace, a marble and gem encrusted, two story double door that opens, as though automatically, as you arrive. You are released and helped down from the buggy by the two slaves. They lead you through the main door and into a side room, where they lock your collar to an eyebolt on the wall. The eyebolt is slightly too high, so your struggle on your toes to stop yourself from being strangled. As your feet tire, the collar bites into your neck and obstructs your breathing. It's not easy to find a comfortable position with your elbows fixed behind you but eventually you learn to twist your neck slightly to one side, which allows a little less pressure, and for your feet to be almost flat on the stone floor.

Day turns to dusk, turns to night. You must be dehydrated still from the long day in the field because you do not feel the urge to piss. You wonder what will happen. Surely the Sultan will not have selected you just to be chained to the wall like an ornament. Eventually the two slaves come back, dragging a bench on one metre high legs. The bench is rounded on its upper surface and in the middle is fixed a butt plug. The plug is a fierce looking gadget with a bulb the size of a fist, and a slightly less wide neck. The tip narrows to a point. You presume this will go into your arse but seriously wonder if you will be able to accommodate the monster.

The slaves release you from the wall and guide you towards the bench. They slather grease on the butt plug and up your arse. They work quietly and confidently and it's obvious to you that they have done this many times before. They are a handsome, white couple with a defined physique, enhanced by their tight fitting harnesses. Their cocks hang down, then you notice that they are wearing PA rings that are padlocked to guiches, which prevent any erection. They must suppress any erotic desire or their erecting cocks will pull against their PA rings and the guiches.

The slaves move your legs either side of the bench so that your arse is directly over the butt plug. Slowly they force you down on the plug, which at first sinks in easily. The slaves move you up and down, up and down, each time pushing you slightly further onto the plug and each time stretching your arse. With accomplished skill they ease you past the widest part of the bulb of the plug and all the way down onto the bench. Your arse clamps around the neck but your notice that this is still as wide as most plugs you have taken in Europe. Soon your arse relaxes and enjoys the fulfilling feeling.

With equal efficiency the slaves tie your feet together, then up to a fixture on the underside of the bench. There is no way you can extract yourself from the plug, nor even relieve the pressure in your arse. Further ropes fix the rod behind your elbows to the sides, and ropes front and back fix your metal collar to the bench and above to a beam. You are completely immobile on the plug, chained and gagged and with no option but to just sit there and suffer. To add further discomfort, the slaves tie a rope around your balls then pull the rope forwards to the front of the bench, stretching them painfully. The slaves stand back to survey their work, then kneel behind you, hands behind their backs, heads bowed, in silence.

The Sultan enters the room in a flurry of robes. Standing before you he surveys the spectacle.

'You will remain plugged for the night, after which I anticipate you will be wide enough to accommodate my cock and anything else I should want to insert. If you need to piss, do so; the slaves will clean it up. If your arse tightens again in the future, you will spend more time on the butt plug. You may spend more time on it anyway, if it pleases me to see you suffer.'

He beckons to one slave, who immediately gets to his feet and follows him out of the room. The other slave lies down, naked, on the bare tiles. All you can do is stare in front and contemplate the plug and the pain in your balls. It is not too long before the pressure in your arse causes it to tighten around the plug, but it is unable to do so. Try as you will, nothing can prevent the cycle of pressure and spasm. Within a few hours, as though your arse has learned its lesson, it fails to tighten further, and just accepts the plug. Within a few more hours all you feel is a dull fullness in your arse, which is not unpleasant. At this time, even your balls are numb and it's only when you subconsciously try to move, that you are made aware of the pressure in your balls.

You try to sleep, but as you doze off and slump, the pressure from your rigid collar awakens you. You maintain your posture so as to limit pressure from the collar, but eventually reach an equilibrium between posture and rest, tolerating some pressure for a little relaxation. The night grinds on. It is warm and although you were sweating earlier from the effort of the plug, you remain comfortable. The slave sleeps, without blanket and effortlessly. After what seems an eternity but is probably only a couple of hours you feel the urge to piss. You grunt to alert the slave but he fails to wake. Eventually the piss flows freely, onto the bench then splashes onto the floor. Only when the slave is splashed with piss does he wake and immediately get to work. He retrieves a cloth from a cupboard and wipes up the piss, being careful to wipe the floor with sweet smelling cleaner, to obscure the smell of the piss. He rapidly returns to sleep and you, your reverie.

Silence is all around you. Moonlight enters the room through upper windows and you can make out gilt encrusted window frames and ornate fittings. Marble and tiles are the predominant wall and floor surfaces, with the occasional Persian rug and cushion on the floor. Clearly, the slave dare not avail himself of these luxuries.

Dawn comes slowly, preceded by footsteps in adjacent rooms. As light begins to filter through the upper windows, the slave awakes and with a sponge proceeds to wash you. He rubs oil over your now sunburned skin as best he can through your bonds. Shortly the Sultan enters, alone but with the same air of authority and determination he demonstrated earlier. He nods to the slave, who unlocks your gag and releases you arms, before continuing to oil you in places not yet reached. You are relieved at the use of your mouth again but it feels dirty and stale. The slave offers you a mouthwash, which you keenly use, spitting the waste into the brass bowl he also offers.

The slave unties your feet and balls and releases the ropes fixing your neck. You gingerly place your feet on the ground. At a command from the Sultan the slave commences to help you off the butt plug. At first it appears stuck but as the slave urges you up and down it is clear that the wider part of the plug is stretching your arse again. You push up with your feet, at the same time push your bowels to dislodge the plug. With a sudden surge of pain the plug plops out and you stand free of the bench. The slave holds you in position for a few minutes while you regain your balance at the same time he wipes your arse of the grease and accumulated secretions. He quickly fixes the chain between your ankles and padlocks your wrist cuffs together at the front. He leads you into a side room, where a toilet beckons you to take a shit. The plug had removed the desire to shit but as soon as you sit on the toilet, out it all comes and it is a huge relief to be rid of it. With your hands locked in front you are unable to wipe yourself but no matter, the slave advances with a douche and proceeds to ram it up your arse and pour water in. Three times he cleans you out until you are passing crystal clear water, and only then does he wipe your arse. You sit a while to make sure every drop is out of your bowel and then the slave leads you back to the room.

The Sultan is lounging naked on a large cushion and motions for the slave to prepare you. You notice the Sultan's cock is erect and huge, like something out of a Tom of Finland cartoon. The slave pushes you over the bench, anchoring your spread ankles to the floor and your hands over the bench to a fixture on the other side. He attaches a short chain to your collar and steps back. The Sultan inspects your arse, applies grease to it and a condom to his cock and proceeds to fuck you. In order to get better penetration he grabs the chain and pulls your neck and head back, obstructing your airway and effectively preventing any noise. All you can do is grunt between thrusts and pray that it will soon be over. It is, but not because he has come, he removes his cock and the condom then proceeds to fuck you in the mouth. The huge cock stretches your jaw to the max but notwithstanding the pain, you are terrified in case you scratch his cock with your teeth. He pummels your head mercilessly and you gag repeatedly, retching and dribbling and gasping for breath when he withdraws. He finishes by masturbating over your head and cum dribbles round your head and onto the floor.

Exhausted, the slave releases you, wipes you down and bids you follow him. With hands still padlocked in front and ankles chained, you shuffle after him, down stairs to a large room where other slaves are eating. They are naked and appear to be free of bonds, except for their metal neck collars. They glance up at you jealously when you enter. The slave fixes your wrists above your head to an eyebolt on the wall and feeds you porridge. Other slaves regard you mockingly. You are sure they know what has been happening over the past 24 hours. Your prominent position, strung up in the mess, being fed, leads you to suspect that they are mere drones in this hive of slaves, working all day and not engaged in pleasing the Sultan at night. What can you do? You relish your humiliation, your taut body stretched out in front of them, your sunburn and your bonds.

You wonder what the day has in store. More sex? More manual labour? Or just restraint and incarceration? As the other slave file out of the mess, the slave releases you and takes you to a waiting buggy, where the ponies glance at you suspiciously. The slave takes you back to the stable, where the other slaves are being kitted up for further pony work or field labour. After releasing your hands and wrists, the slave hands you over to the keepers and disappears.

PART 15

Your collar is attached to a chain on the wall and you are unceremoniously dumped onto the hay where you find Dale, who, notwithstanding a few bruises, is smiling. Slaves who have been rented out the previous evening have a half-day rest, he tells you quietly. Since you had no sleep the previous night, this seems like an unparalleled luxury. The other slaves leave the stable, as ponies or farm labourers, leaving Dale and yourself and a couple of other slaves chained to the wall, but otherwise free of bonds.

The other two slaves drift rapidly off to sleep while you tell your experiences to Dale. He is reticent to tell you what had happened to him; he was harshly treated, tied up by his wrists to an overhead beam, whipped, paddled, subject to electric shocks then fucked. He spent the night in a tight hogtie, gagged with and O-ring, plugged, and was periodically fucked in the mouth and used as a urinal throughout the night. All this seemed within the bounds of acceptable slave use by the fraternity and no one made a fuss if you return, on time, with only a few bruises.

You reach over and massage Dale's bruises and aching shoulders. He rests his head on your chest while you caress his back and nipples. You reach down into the straw and grab his cock, against which he masturbates, quickly spurting cum under the straw. No one is around and it seems that the event has gone unnoticed. Dale nestles further into the curve of your body and you lean down to kiss his forehead, his eyes, his lips. He rests his hand between your thighs but quickly falls asleep. You pull him further to you and you sleep in each other's embrace.

You startle awake as shouting fills the stable. The ponies are returning after their morning work. They are all sweating and panting and some have whip marks on their shoulders. The keepers quickly disengage them from their harnesses, gags, tails and chains and hang them by their wrists for showering. You and Dale also get sprayed with cold water and attempt to wash the dirt and straw from your bodies. Porridge is served, as before, and the pony slaves are allowed to rest for 30 minutes.

Another afternoon in the fields looms as the keepers return to chain everyone into groups of four and march you off. You are chained next to Dale and each of you cast furtive glances and smile whenever the keepers are not looking. Having a friend like Dale seems to make staying here so much more worthwhile. He is the tallest of all the white slaves and his stunning physique catches the eye of all the other slaves. You watch his muscles ripple and relax as he tills the soil and harvests the potatoes. The sweat glistens on his tanned skin and runs in rivulets down the small of his back and into his arse. The afternoon passes quickly as you consider a future next to Dale. If only it can be so.

Days turn to weeks, which turn to months. Your only clue is the moon, which slowly fills, then disappears. The weather hardly changes, neither does the routine. Pony work in the mornings, field work in the afternoons. The evening lottery of who gets chosen for auction favours the white slaves, but this is accepted by the other slaves without rancour. Hell, they get a good night's sleep while you are getting flogged and getting your arse plugged; why would they complain? Two nights a week you service the Sultan, who seems less inclined to impale you on the butt plug, but have you in his bedroom where he can restrain and fuck you. Before he goes to sleep his attaches your collar or nose ring by a chain to the wall of the bedroom.

Several months after your arrival and after the afternoon's work, you trudge back to the stable, shower, eat porridge and settle down next to Dale on the straw. No sooner have you collapsed onto the straw than you are both taken to a room at the side of the auction room. The Sultan's slaves appear and proceed to padlock your wrists behind your back, then connect then via a short chain to the back of your neck. Your head is forced back. Your ankles are manacled as before and the slaves then tie your balls tightly, forcing them to the depths of your ball sack. A chain is attached to the ball rope. You notice that Dale's huge balls are stretched down some 4 cm, and he winces as more rope and the chain are applied. Lockable pecker gags are inserted in both of you. Your cock stands to attention revealing your excitement.

The Sultan enters and walks straight up to you both.

'I have decided to buy you both. I have a passion for good looking white men and you two are the best of the present bunch. I earmarked you from early reports from Europe,' he says, pointing to you. 'I have watched you both working hard as ponies and in the fields and am pleased with the results. I have paid a fortune to the slave trader so expect to get my money's worth. You two, and these two slaves here, will be in my inner circle of slaves. The rest you see at my palace are the drones, who work in the palace and garden, but may not enter the inner sanctum. You will be by my side at all times, attending my every personal need. You will bath me, dress me, feed me, be my footstool and offer yourselves unfailingly when I need sadistic sex. I am a ruthless, but safe, sadist. If you are marked it will not be for long. You both have nipple rings and pierced nasal septums, which is good. I may use these rings to anchor you down when I use you. Now go to the buggy.'

The slaves grab your balls chains and lead you to the waiting buggy. There are now two poles on the buggy and you are both attached by your neck collars and with wide belts around your chests and legs, so that no movement is possible. The ponies heave and groan as you take off up the hill. The extra weight causes them to slip and stumble and the Sultan uses his whip to beat them into further effort.

You reach the palace and are led into the room where you had been impaled. It is bare apart from the bench with its butt plug. You are both relieved of your bonds, except the gag, which remains in place. Dale eyes the bench suspiciously and eases himself towards you, for protection is seems. You plead with your eyes for him to be still but he is grabbed by the two slaves and dragged to the bench. He knows better than to struggle and as he stands beside the bench, he glances at you, tears welling up in his eyes. It is less than 24 hours since he was fucked by a renter and he is sure this is going to hurt.

The two slaves ease him over the butt plug, with a leg either side of the bench. They apply copious amounts of grease to the plug and his arse, then indicate that he should try to impale himself. Dale slowly eases himself down but stops half way as his arse refuses to take any more. The slaves grab his arms and start moving him up and down, up and down, as they did with you before. Slowly he sinks lower and lower onto the plug but is still to take the widest part. The slaves hold him as far down as he can go for two minutes, then with one shove, force him down onto the bench. Dale yelps into the gag but only a muffled 'mmmph' comes out. As his arse closes around the neck of the plug he settles down, even lifting his feet slightly to test the pressure. You think he might even be smiling behind that gag.

The slaves tie his wrists, feet, neck and balls as you were before. You then appreciate the stunning feature before you; immobile on a plug, chest thrust forwards and glistening with sweat, hands pulled up and balls pulled forwards. You want to go and hug him but dare not move. The slaves fuss around and clean up the area, leaving Dale in the middle of the floor, in a beam of late afternoon light.

The slaves then turn their attention to you. They push you to the floor on your front then pull your arms back between your legs. One slave gets a set of double eight metal cuffs that fix your wrists and ankles together at the same spot. Your arms are pulled painfully between your legs but you cannot move. The pecker gag is unlocked and an O-ring gag inserted. With you arse in the air and your mouth fixed open, you can only imagine what will happen.

The slaves retreat to the shadows as the Sultan and another Arab enter the room. They go straight up to you, fingering your arse and mouth as you squirm to accommodate their invading digits. Your arse responds automatically by clamping down on the fingers and your tongue caresses the fingers in your mouth. The Arabs are pleased with the response and quickly shed their robes. You are amazed at the physique of the Arabs and their huge erections attest to their state of arousal. They quickly don condoms and whilst the Sultan fucks your arse, the other Arabs lies back and guides your open mouth over and onto his cock. Your position does not allow you to do anything, other than to go down on the cock. You are impaled, as much in the mouth as by the cock up your arse. The 'mouth fucking' Arab moves your head up and down, so that you gag whenever his cock reaches the back of your throat, and dribble at the other extreme. Meanwhile the Sultan drills away at your arse. You are amazed at the stamina of the Sultan, who had already fucked a slave once that day, but within a few minutes he tenses, shudders and thrusts deeply. His cock languishes in its warm hole, while the mouth fucker grinds away. His cock swells to enormous proportions and intermittently cuts off your airway, but soon you detect a shortening of his thrusts, giving way to a powerful deep thrust, which sends you into a fit of gagging. He holds your head with his cock buried up to the hilt while he shoots his load.

Without speaking, they both disengage from your holes and leave. The slaves return to clean and release you. You notice they both have erections and suspect they were watching proceedings from the shadows. Probably they had seen it all before. With you cleaned up they reattach the ankle and wrist chains and attach your metal collar by a chain to the bench, leaving you enough room to lie down or walk around the bench. They place a bucket containing water, and a sponge beside you. One of them speaks softly,

'You are to look after him tonight. Clean up any mess. No one will be here. If you try to release him you will both spend the next two days on the plug. We advise you don't disobey the Sultan.'

This new responsibility leaves you somewhat shocked. Since pledging your life to Masters in England and Europe you were not given the opportunity to take any responsibility for anything. You were told to do things and beaten if you messed up. You were told to avail yourself sexually at all times, which you did almost without effort now. But you had not been told to care for someone or something, which implied a certain degree of trust and confidence. You were hardly likely to escape, being chained by the neck to the heavy bench, on which Dale was impaled, but your hands, although chained, were free to do whatever you wanted; a truly new experience.

The slaves pad silently out of the room and you view Dale in the fading light. His skin glows and is stretched tautly over his bound body. The gag prevents him from speaking but he utters gentle groans, almost purring. It's early hours yet and you are sure the pain of the butt plug and discomfort on his immobile neck and balls will soon cause a different sound from him.

You circle Dale and his eyes follow. Your hands caress his smooth, wet skin and you massage his shoulders and back. He responds by pressing into your hands, as best he can. His cock springs to attention, creating further tension on his balls. Your hands travel down his back and locate his arse, now stretched by the plug. You massage around his arse, hoping that it will relax further to accommodate the plug, and he groans with gratitude. His cock remains rigid and with one hand massaging his arse, the other pumps his cock. You are careful not to create additional tension on his stretched balls but it is obvious from his throbbing cock that he wants release. As your fingers play around the tip of his cock he shoots a load over the bench and onto the floor. As he cums you sense his arse tightening around the plug. Sweat drips from Dale as his cock jerks in the dying throws of orgasm. Two deep grunts sound like 'thank you' and his eyes brim with happiness.

With your mouth, you suck residual cum from his cock, sucking it to make sure every last drop is out. This causes further spasms of delight from Dale. With the sponge you clean the cum off the floor and wipe his sweaty body as best you can. The cool water is blissful to him and he moves slightly to enable you to wipe around his cock and arse. You drape your shackled arms around his torso and rest your head in his crotch. You love this man.

Eventually, you must rest and sink to the hard floor to sleep. Dale is wide-awake but there is nothing more you can do to make him comfortable. His eyes glisten in the moonlight, but the room is otherwise dark. Like you, he must suffer this ordeal, impaled on the plug, gagged and tightly bound, with balls cruelly stretched, all night. Your heart goes out to him and you hope he receives your love.

The night passes and you sleep fitfully. You are awakened by Dale pissing on the floor and move to clean it up. His open eyes and erection demand your attention and you move to suck his beautiful cock. He purrs and you gently massage his cock with your lips and tongue. You force your head down as far as it will go and sense his cock respond accordingly. He cannot push his cock forwards but within a few minutes, shoots a small load down your throat. You suck all the cum out of his cock and he jerks with delight.

Leaving his cock you slide your tongue up his belly, licking the sweat off as you go. His nipples are erect and your mouth chews gently on each one in turn. He groans in ecstasy and you sense him relax in his bonds. With your fingers you find his plugged arse again and massage it. With your mouth chewing on his nipples and your finger on his arse, he seems to drift into a state of erotic bliss, only opening his eyes when his immobilised collar obstructs his breathing. He visibly relaxes and seems to enjoy his bound state, in contrast to your night of transfixed agony.

For hours you make love to Dale. His cock oozes precum and occasionally you use your mouth to clean it away. As dawn approaches you lie on the floor to get some sleep before the day's activities begin. As the daylight percolates the upper windows, Dale grunts, then pisses again. Once again you clean up the mess and wash him down. As you finish, the two slaves enter and complement you on keeping Dale clean and the floor shiny. They lead you over to the wall and attach your manacled wrists high up and apart and your ankles similarly spread apart on the floor. They padlock your collar to an eyebolt on the wall so that you are effectively fixed to the wall. They turn their attention to Dale and after releasing his gag and bound body, slowly lower his feet to the ground and ease him from the butt plug. Thanks to the massaging, he extracts himself easily from the plug, then stands and stretches his aching body. They push him to a kneeling position and he puts his hands behind his back and with eyes cast down, and awaits his fate.

The Sultan, watching these proceedings from the shadows, strides up to Dale.

'I like a slave who knows how to behave, even when his Master is not around. You don't know, but I was watching the two of you last night through a peephole in the wall. I am excited by two white men making love to each other and now it is your turn to make love to slave number one.'

He urges Dale forwards and he kneels, hands behind his back, in front of you. Your cock, sensing his presence, immediately comes to attention and the Sultan urges Dale's mouth onto it. Dale works his mouth expertly, using his tongue to create extra pressure points along the shaft. He purposely makes himself gag by taking your whole cock in, then resumes his up and down sucking which has you ejaculate into his mouth within minutes.

The Sultan watches and, visibly excited by the spectacle, sheds his clothes and lies on a large cushion. The two slaves work automatically to place pillows behind his head and back. One slave releases you whilst the other brings both of you to the Sultan.

'I expect to be pleasured by you two whenever I demand. You will learn to massage my body, nibble my nipples, suck my cock and finger and lick my arse at any time of the day or night. For now you, number one, can get your arse over my cock and sit on it, whilst you, number two, can suck and chew my nipples.' After placing a condom on his cock, you ease your arse down over it. It is certainly no smaller than yesterday and you struggle to accommodate it. As you move up and down, up and down, your arse relaxes and starts to enjoy the sensation. Meanwhile Dale keenly chews away on the Sultan's nipples, enjoying the musky odour of his body and the rubbery nature of his erect nipples. The Sultan closes his eyes and is in heaven. One slave massages his shoulders whilst the other massages his thighs. One Master, four slaves working in unison towards nirvana. Dale increases the pressure from his teeth on the Sultan's nipples and he seems to enjoy this. As Dale works harder and harder the Sultan stiffens and fills the condom up your arse with cum. You both know to ease up after the Sultan has ejaculated and you let him down slowly from his plateau of ecstasy.

As you disengage yourselves, the two slaves wash the Sultan and return his clothing. Another slave, obviously a low order drone, enters with a trolley of food, and four separate bowls for the slaves. You are instructed to feed the Sultan a mixture of breads, fruit and dates and to prepare strong coffee. He turns to address the slaves,

'I am pleased with my quartet of slaves. Serve me well and you will be cared for. Disobey me and you will be returned to the stables,' he says in a tone which leaves no question unanswered.

PART 16

The Sultan leaves and the two slaves eat from their bowls of fruit and bread, and help themselves to coffee and fruit juice. The two of you do likewise and relish the difference to the regular slave food in the stable. The two slaves, who had unpronounceable Eastern European names, urge you to pick up the dishes and follow them. It is their job to teach you, in a mixture of broken English and sign language, all they know about serving the Sultan. They teach you how to prepare his clothes, how to clean his slippers, how to arrange his table and how to bath him. It seems the Sultan does nothing for himself. He has four naked, white slaves to look after his every need. The two slaves explain that the Sultan likes to watch boys struggle on the butt plug, so each night one of you will be fixed onto it. They have spent many nights on the plug. If the Sultan thinks you are too comfortable, he will have a larger plug installed; he has a vast collection of plugs of different shapes and sizes. Also, if he thinks your arse it too tight, he will order you impaled during the day. He enjoys watching the slaves play with each other and he noted that you two have an obvious affection for each other, so was keen to acquire you both.

The Sultan has little to do with the common rabble in the town, who rent slaves and beat and sexually abuse them. He thinks you get better service if you look after a slave. Most of the drones in this house were once favoured slaves, but they let themselves down by some indiscretion and were returned to the stable for rehabilitation, before being readmitted as drones to the palace.

'First thing, we get those cuffs off. Ugly things,' says one of the slaves, and leads you both outside to a foundry beside the house. A huge, hairy, black slave wielding a metal cutter saws through your wrist and ankle cuffs, being careful to protect your skin in the process. Your arms feel weightless without those heavy cuffs and your feet feel like dancing. Dale too smiles when the weights are lifted from his limbs. Cutting the metal neck collars off is particularly difficult but once it is removed, your head feels unsteady without its support. Now, absolutely naked except for the nose ring, nipples rings and PA ring, you massage your wrists, ankles and neck. The white lines on your wrists and ankles and around your neck illustrate just how tanned you have become during your enslavement and forced labour outdoors. A badge of service, you surmise.

The black slave picks up two bright, shiny metal collars, at which point you realise you will not be permitted to be entirely unshackled. The collars are of stainless steel with a sunken tightening and locking screw, the key to which is a complex hexagonal arrangement. He places the collar around your neck, and with the key, slowly tightens it. The metal bends slightly as the ends come together. He tightens it so that it is constricting the blood supply to your head, then backs off a few notches until it fits snugly, but without any space, around your neck. The collar has four D fixtures welded to the front, back and sides, presumable for attaching chains, padlocks and other items of restraint. When the black slave is happy with the result, he spot-welds the collar closed, so even if you had a key, you would not be able to open it.

You sit down and Dale takes his place for fitting. He is smiling and accepts the new collar eagerly. You look like twins, tall, tanned, well-built naked young white men, happy in your enslavement. The two slaves urge you to follow them and they lead you both to a bathroom. The gold and white tiled room has two shower nozzles in the middle and the table to one side has an array of toiletries. One slave tells you to shave, which you do keenly, as the three days growth was starting to irritate your face. They then sit you on a chair and start to shave your head. The fuzz that was starting to grow was equally irritating and you were glad to see it go. They also shave your cock, balls and arse, stating that the Sultan wants all these areas shaved twice a week. The remainder of your body is covered only in fine hair and hardly shows. Dale too, sensing the joy that you showed, was keen to be shaved and together you then enter the shower and enjoy the pleasure of washing each other all over.

The rest of the day is spent practicing those everyday tasks to care for the Sultan. Occasionally he will call one of you over to do some menial task, make tea, clear away dishes, offer yourself as a footstool or pour him a drink. At other times, if he wants you around, you will kneel beside him, hands behind your back and gaze averted downwards.

Towards the evening he likes watching two of his personal slaves play with each other. He enjoys the tenderness they show, and when they fuck or suck, he fixes his attention on the face of the top and watches him drift off into heaven. The slaves who are not playing are engaged in playing with the Sultan's nipples and cock, being careful not to bring him to orgasm. The Sultan would invariably fuck one or both slaves whilst watching the other two play, and if his friends are around, it is a free-for-all of sucking and fucking.

After playtime, you clean up any mess and prepare for the evening meal. While the Sultan eats, you assume the slave's position by his side, until needed. While he rests after dinner, you eat your own meal, usually a more basic version of what he has just had. If a slave is earmarked for the butt plug treatment, they are hand cuffed and gagged and held down while the other slaves give him a series of enemas, until the water runs clean. They are then positioned near the bench, awaiting the arrival of the Sultan who supervises the lowering of the slave onto the butt plug. Records are kept of which plug is used on which slave, so that each time a slave is destined for this torture, only the same or a larger plug is used.

Tonight it is the turn of one of the Eastern European slaves to spend the night on the butt plug. He protests only slightly before realising that there is no escape. He is slightly smaller that you and you wonder, when you see the size of the butt plug, how he will accommodate it. His partner assures you that this is his normal sized plug and indeed, as the Sultan watches, the slave, with a little assistance from the rest of the slave team, swallows the plug easily and without obvious distress. His partner stays to look after him during the night while you and Dale tend to domestic duties and pleasure the Sultan.

The Sultan's bedroom is a vast affair. In the middle of the marbled room is a four-poster bed, the posts of which are festooned with eyebolts and chains. Chains hang from the ceiling above the bed. Small tables beside the bed are covered with ropes, cuffs of various descriptions, condoms and lube. Butt plugs and dildos line up against the wall like miniature soldiers. Whips and paddles hang from hooks on the wall and gags - O-ring gags, pecker gags, muzzles and lots of rolls of duct tape, crowd another table at the end of the bed.

The Sultan pushes Dale to his knees at the side of the bed and pushes you to the end of the bed. He spreads your legs and fastens your ankles to chains attached to the corner of the bed. He stands on the bed and fastens your wrists to cuffs on the chains high up at the corners of the bed. He attaches chains to the side D fixtures of your collar so that, as well as being spread-eagled, you can no longer move your head. He clips a parachute around your ball sac and pulls it down to an eyebolt on the floor, stretching your balls and further limiting movement. Into your mouth he ties an O-ring gag.

The Sultan turns his attention to Dale, who is stealing glances at your preparations from the corner of his eyes. He cuffs Dale's hand behind his back and pulls him to the end of the bed, directly in line with your arse.

'Clean his arse number 2. I don't want to see any mess there when I come to it,' he commands.

Dale approaches your arse, gingerly at first then with vigour. He dips his tongue into your crack and forces it into your arse hole. He licks it, sucks it and digs his tongue into it. As best you can, you push your arse towards Dale, but very little movement is possible. Meanwhile, the Sultan mounts the bed and thrusts his condom-covered cock into your mouth and into the depths of your throat. You try not to gag but are unable to move your head and just heave and choke. Again and again he thrusts his cock and you gasp to breathe between thrusts. You try to concentrate on Dale rimming your arse, but each pounding of your head demands your attention.

Eventually, the Sultan slows his thrusting and, dripping with sweat, turns his attention to your arse. At the same time he commands Dale to fuck your mouth. Dale mounts the bed and gently obeys, but his style is heavenly compared to that of the Sultan's. He eases in and out and round and about and rather than gagging you with deep thrusts, he slowly pushes his cock in, so that you feel as though you are swallowing the whole man. Dale purposely maintains a slow pace, so that precum juice lubricates your mouth and mixes with your spit. When he ejaculates it's a beautifully smooth mixture that spurts down your throat and which you swallow keenly. At the other end the Sultan bangs away with his bulbous dick. Your arse must be used to this by now because it relaxes to take it all in and you are hardly in any pain. He pumps his sperm into the condom up your arse and unceremoniously plops out, leaving your arse gaping and wanting.

Rather than release you, the Sultan lowers your arms and cuffs them behind your back. He replaces the O-ring gag with a ball gag, then turns his attention to Dale. Dale is fitted with the O-ring gag and is cuffed with hands behind him. The Sultan lies on his bed and pulls Dale between his legs, fixing his cock in Dale's mouth. By ropes attached to Dale's collar and around his waist, the Sultan fixes Dale's head onto his cock. Dale cannot withdraw his head and the Sultan's cock remains in his mouth. The Sultan drifts off to sleep. You can do nothing but watch Dale with his mouth full of the Sultan's cock, and Dale can only look at the Sultan's pubic hair and swallow his cock.

Periodically the Sultan's cock stiffens and Dale gasps for breath as it fills his mouth. But the Sultan sleeps on. You are unable to sleep, aroused at the sight of Dale's torture and by the pressure on your collar when you change position. You are a furniture accessory, an erotic life sculpture to decorate the Sultan's bedroom, and a convenient and accepting fuck hole for whoever avails himself.

An ornate, gold clock chimes the hours and this makes the night seem interminably long. At midnight the Sultan awakes and releases the two of you, only to padlock your nose rings and collars to eyebolts on the wall and leave you locked and cuffed on the hard floor for the rest of the night. Although you are touching Dale, your padlocked noses and necks and cuffed wrists prevent any more meaningful affection. Instead you intertwine legs and slowly drift off to sleep.

PART 17

Life develops a routine. Cleaning and domestic chores during the day, interspersed with the occasional sexual abuse, especially if there are visitors. In the evening, it's either sex play in the bedroom, impalement on the butt plug or looking after Dale on the butt plug. If the Sultan is visiting other households he will usually take two slaves. These escort slaves are shaven, given a hot bath and smothered in fragrant oil, plugs are fixed in their arses and they are fitted with a full body harness with attached chastity devices, which lock their cocks in a cage-like structure. Pecker gags are locked in and hands are cuffed behind backs.

The Sultan enters the guest's house pulling the slaves with a chain attached to their collars. The Sultan is proud of his good-looking slaves and wants to show them off. You and Dale certainly enjoy these evenings, where your sole role is to appear handsome but untouchable, lying or kneeling at the Sultan's feet, the ultimate fashion accessory.

Certainly your life is better than that of the many drones, ponies and field slaves, who toil day after day and are rented out at night. Occasionally you hear that one has fallen sick, or become too old and unattractive, whereupon they have been returned to their country or origin, to find a new life on the streets. What your new life also gives you is time to think. Time to think about your European Masters and what they are up to. As the weeks go by you become certain that they have forgotten all about you. Just another slave, lost to the great slave trade, about which governments seem to know, or care, little. What is actually happening however is quite different.

Master Ian's army friends, led by the rough looking German SAS officer called Hans, have scoured maps, the internet and navigation charts to find the best way to spring you out of the desert. The airport seems the best bet; it is isolated and can be approached quietly from the desert. It seems unmanned and is within easy reach of the town. They have pinpointed several likely buildings, the castle, some of the larger houses, including the Sultan's palace, which is prominent on the hill. Satellite images suggest slave activities with people working long hours in the fields and human pony traffic on the roads. The only question that remains is when to put the plan into action.

Hans' contacts with the European air defence systems indicate a couple of rarely used transport planes in Italy, which would not be missed for a couple of days. He secretly gets them air-worthy and after a few test runs gets them configured to take a total of four vehicles. The vehicles are armed and spacious, but fast. A mock up of the desert strip, the road and the town, with its key locations, is constructed in an army training ground in Italy, and several practice runs serve to iron out strategic problems with communication and transport. The team will land quietly, move straight into town and plough straight into the houses likely to hold slaves. They will call your name over a loudspeaker and hope that you are able to come to them. If not, that someone will indicate where you are. They will capture important looking people and hold them as hostages until you are located and safely put on the plane. All this is achieved without anyone, least of all local governments in Europe, knowing. All personnel are sworn to secrecy, on peril of an extensive period of imprisonment, at best! The personnel know that would be no ordinary prison, but one which Hans has personal authority over.

You, of course, know nothing of this. As the days pass, you resign yourself to your situation. You seem to have two lives here. One, the obvious one, the life of a slave. The other, as a lover to Dale, who freely admits his love for you. You are rarely out of each others sight and although you are often forced to abuse each other, you do it and accept it willingly and lovingly. Your heart aches when he is in pain and he comforts you, when possible, when you are being tortured. Fortunately, the Sultan sees this growing affection and rarely separates you both. Rather he will plan to make you suffer at either his hand or the hands of trusted friends. He likes watching the two of you caress and fuck each other; a kind of benign voyeurism. One part of you wants to return to Europe but the other part would hate to be parted from Dale. Fortunately, that is not a question you ever think you will have to deal with, as both rescue and escape seem impossible.

Weeks turn to months, the weather becomes cooler, but never does any rain fall. The town gardens always look green from watering from the underground aquifers, and the countless hours of slave labour spent attending them. The town hums along. No one visits from the outside and no one leaves. It's as though the town is a utopia in the middle of the desert. Why would people leave when life is so perfect?

When you are not servicing the Sultan and not chained up, Dale and you try to keep fit by doing callisthenics, lifting heavy furniture around and doing push-ups. Certainly there was not an ounce of fat to be found on either of you. You also spend time massaging fragrant oils into each other so that you both glow, and this pleases the Sultan greatly. The other two East European slaves struggle to match your physiques and, whilst they equal your physical training efforts, they never quite match your physical appearances. They worry more and more that they will be relegated to the drone class, and their places taken by prettier slaves. However, the Sultan is a reasonable man and he values devotion to duty as well as physical appearance. The competition did, however, keep the other slaves on their toes.

The Sultan is very cunning, in having a hierarchy amongst his slaves, and slaves were very much aware that they could slide up or down in his favour. Extra effort to enhance physique, or present an attractive dinner setting, would curry favour and may earn a night in the Sultan's bedroom. A sloppy effort in the garden, or dragging of feet whilst hauling the buggy, may result in being chained to the dungeon wall for a week and flogged every day.

You certainly have no desire to return to the drudgery of working the fields, although you did find hauling the buggy erotic. But whilst you maintain your position at the top of the slave ladder, you were dammed well going to keep it. Together, Dale and you work to keep fit, look good and predict the Sultan's every need. You both offer yourselves willingly to his sexual urges, and those of his guests, and if this means spending the odd night on the butt plug, then so be it. You wonder if this is as good as it will get, if this is to be the rest of your life. You wonder what will happen to you when you get older and became less attractive. Will you be cast out, to the fields with the other drones, or will the Sultan send you home, penniless, to live on the streets of Europe? Some things did not bear thinking about too deeply.

PART 18

The planes glide noiselessly towards the desert airstrip and Hans notes that everything is as it appeared on the satellite photos and maps. It is nighttime and there are no lights around the strip, the plane uses infrared imaging and auto gadgetry to slide onto the desert strip. At the parking bay, soldiers and personnel deplane and commence unloading vehicles from the transport plane. Each car carries six personnel and is armed with automatic guns. A handful of soldiers secure the planes and airstrip and the remaining 24 set off to town in the vehicles. There are no lights on the vehicles. The drivers know the way by heart from the numerous trial runs at the training ground, and the full moon provides more than enough light.

One vehicle heads straight to the castle. The unarmed guards are thrown to the side as the vehicle plunges through the gate and into the courtyard. Soldiers spread out into the castle and adjacent buildings. Two men go straight to the master bedroom, smash through the door and lunge at the body in the bed. The slave trader is hardly awake when he is cuffed and dragged naked into the courtyard. Residents of other bedrooms are similarly cuffed and dragged as they are, with and without clothes, to the courtyard. The slave trader is tied, by a rope around his neck, to a central column, and others are forced to a kneeling position around him. Some twenty Arabs are subsequently cuffed, kneeling and trembling in the courtyard. Some are naked and struggle to cover their cocks, but this is impossible. The slave trader is completely exposed and humiliated.

Two soldiers stumble across the dungeon and adjacent stable and are astounded at the sight of up to twenty naked men, all with nose rings, chained by their necks to walls. To say that the slaves are startled is an understatement. The sight of two armed, white soldiers bursting into their area is not within their past experience. The keepers, who were outside asleep, are dragged into the stable and thrown to the ground. At this point the slaves realise they are being released. The soldiers waste no time in persuading the keepers to locate the keys and release the slaves, after which the keepers are cuffed and dragged out, with chains around their necks, to join the others in the courtyard. The slaves, somewhat bewildered by all this activity and freedom, follow and crouch down along the wall of the courtyard.

A soldier discovers the kitchen and ushers a few, then all the slaves there to feast on whatever they can find. The slaves eat their fill and whilst some pig out and vomit, most can manage only a small amount of the rich food. They stumble back to the courtyard and collapse against the back wall. Very few feel the urge to vent their anger at the bound Arabs in the courtyard, and after a few perfunctory slaps and kicks, join their colleagues against the wall. This behaviour amazes the soldiers, who initially feared for the lives of the keepers and Arab Masters. Some slaves actually offer food to their captive Arab Masters.

Other teams move rapidly to other houses in the town and apprehend anyone who looks important, in whatever state they are found. Slaves are released as they are found. The soldiers note a similar bewildering lack of revenge by the slaves. There is a certain peace about the place, without the rejoicing the soldiers had experienced on other prisoner release forays.

The first you are aware that anything is untoward is when you are awoken by a crash, as the vehicle plunges through the palace gate and screeches to a halt at the main door. You are cuffed and padlocked by your nose ring to a chain and the floor of the Sultan's bedroom. Dale is spread eagled on the bed on his front, with the Sultan asleep on top of him, having fucked him earlier in the night. The Sultan is barely awake before huge, gloved hands drag him off the bed. One soldier stands on his neck on the floor, another cuffs him and hauls him to his feet. His neck is collared and he is dragged to the side and forced to his knees. The keys to the chain securing your nose ring and cuffs are easily located on the bedside table and you are released. Dale's ropes are untied. He joins you and you cling to each other, not really understanding what is going on. At first you wonder if this is a slave take-over, some other group of traders stealing the Sultan's slaves and leading you to a life of misery. However, your fears are quickly dispelled when you hear German being spoken between the soldiers. You have no idea what they are saying.

'We are from England and America. Will you take us there,' you whisper, pleadingly, to the soldier nearest you.

The soldier swings round to see who is talking English. 'Are you the boy to Masters Mark and Peter in England, and Master Ian in Germany?' he asks in broken English.

'Yes. I was kidnapped from Germany many months ago and brought here. My friend here, Dale, has been her much longer. Will you help us get back?' you ask once again.

'That's what we're here for, to find you and take you home. Fritz!' he yells, 'radio to Hans, we've found him. He's OK.'

'We go together,' you state, staring at the soldier and clutching Dale to you closely. 'Where I go, he goes too.'

'But we've only got instructions to bring you back, no one else.' The soldier seems somewhat bewildered but resolute and immovable.

You grab Dale's hand and drag him to the bed. You sit defiantly on the bed and wrap your arms around Dale. Dale moulds himself into your body and rests his head on your chest.

'Then go away,' you shout, tears forming in your eyes. Dale gently wipes your face and looks into your eyes.

'You go,' says Dale. 'I'll find a way to join you later.'

'They can take both of us or go back empty handed.' You will not be moved.

The soldier grabs the radio from Fritz. 'Sir, the boy's got a friend he wants to bring along. He won't come without him. What do we do?'

You overhear the radio message and strain to hear the reply. 'Ya, ya, is OK. Bring the two of them.'

'You're on boys, get your stuff and we're outta here,' the soldier tells you.

'What stuff? We've been naked for months except for this nose ring and this collar. We own nothing.' You state, without a hint of embarrassment.

'Shit, never thought of bringing clothes. Grab some clothes from this guy. He must have something decent to wear.' The soldier looks doubtful, but you know the Sultan's wardrobe well and lead Dale off to plunder it.

You re-emerge into the room wearing the leather jeans and a leather shirt and knee-high boots, which you were transported in. Dale finds blue jeans and a sweatshirt and boots. Your collars and nose rings glisten. You cast an eye at the Sultan, who grins and almost nods his approval.

The entire entourage marches from the house to the town square. Hundreds of people are gathered, ordinary town folk, naked slaves and bound Arab Masters. In the middle of the square the slave trader and Sultan are cuffed and tied back to back on a platform. Both are naked and more than a few children laugh at the sight of these people, so high and mighty before, now naked, bound and humiliated. Hans, an impressive sight at the gest of times, mounts the platform and a hush sweeps over the crowd.

Hans knows a lot. He has been around Master Ian for many years and has even joined him on a few 'camps', when slaves were being inducted. He is not an active member in the inner circle of Masters and slaves in Germany, but he knows everything that is going on. He has observed the behaviour of slaves in this desert town and notices that they are not full of revenge. Some slaves seem angry at their release but the vast majority sit quietly and respectfully. Some have even offered comfort to their bound Arab Masters and sit close by them.

'Tonight is the start of your new life. For those who were Masters, you are now slaves. For those who were slaves, you are now free,' Hans shouts. 'It is clear that human rights have been abused in this town for a long time. You have knowingly kidnapped people from around the world and held them against their will, in slavery, in sexual slavery. You have mistreated and sexually abused people and this will horrify many nations. This will not continue.' Hans pauses and listens to the silence.

A few slaves mumble in the background and the bound Arabs squirm uncomfortably.

Hans gets the picture. Most slaves here may have been initially bought here under duress, but now they are happy, maybe even happier than they were in their own countries. They probably enjoy some, if not most, of their slavery. The down-turned eyes of the slaves, some even with tears, make Hans revise his plans. He had initially thought to liberate the town and set the slaves free. However, on viewing the situation, a small town in the middle of the desert, he knows that the chances of slaves making their way safely home are nil. Even if he arranges more planes, it's likely that many will refuse to leave.

'I offer you a new life. A life of mutual respect. Those slaves who wish to stay here, either as free men or slaves, may do so. Those who wish to leave, I will take some back now and others will be collected later. For those who wish to stay with their Masters, this will be a relationship of mutual consent; abuse, without consent, will be harshly punished. For those slaves who wish to turn the tables on their former Masters, you will be given the opportunity to do so.

And how will this be enforced, you ask. You will do this because you want to, and because if you don't, I will return, without warning, and level this town. I don't even have to return to do this; we have missiles that will do it for us. In the meantime, I will appoint two slaves to oversee these revised arrangements. Furthermore, the former Masters you see bound before you,' he says, pointing to the Sultan and the slave trader and all the bound former Masters, 'will languish in the dungeon for the foreseeable future. They may be treated as slaves, as they have treated others. If there are abuses of slaves in the town, they will be executed. That will leave you without leading members of your community, which will then disintegrate into chaos. If all goes well, they will be released, but only when I, and a democratically elected group of citizens, agree.

We leave at midday. My soldiers will make arrangements, so now slaves please line up and make your wishes known.'

Hans surveys the crowd. His soldiers are strategically placed and take slaves' names; very few as it turns out, wish to go home. Slaves mostly elect to stay and go to join their bound Masters to inform them of this.

Those bound are marched off to the dungeon where they are stripped and chained by their necks to the dungeon walls. Slaves wander around, looking lost and bewildered. Members of the public take pity on them and ask the slaves to join them in their homes, where they offer them clothing. Most slaves choose to remain naked, collared and ringed, and offer themselves as house slaves, until their Masters are released.

The Sultan and the slave trader are taken to the dungeon with the others but are restrained against the walls by manacles and neck collars. They are left naked and exposed to others, who may wish to abuse them.

PART 19

During the flight back to Europe, Dale nestles in your lap and sleeps. You find it impossible to rest and stare out of the window at the passing clouds and wonder what will happen to those left behind in the desert. You expected that most of the slaves would stay in the desert town, since they came from impoverished countries where many slept on the streets. The chance to stay in the desert town, either as free men or slaves, would seem a wonderful opportunity to most of them. Those with you in the plane now had been harshly treated and bore the scars to prove this. They hated everything about the desert town and never wanted to see it again.

You caress Dale's shaved head and massage his scalp, something he always enjoyed. You expect your European Masters will be pleased to have Dale as an addition to their family and Dale has already told you he likes this idea. You have only one condition for your Masters, that you are allowed to stay with Dale, that you will not be separated for more than a few days, if you are loaned out to other Masters. You suspect the Masters will be very reluctant to loan you out in the future though.

Dale opens his eyes and smiles. He is encased in your leather-clad arms and the smell of leather has always intoxicated him. He reaches up and pulls you down onto him. You kiss long and hard, without the slightest regard for the other slaves and soldiers around you. As you emerge from your embrace you see slaves and soldiers alike smiling at you. Some soldiers have 'adopted' slaves, who nestle against their legs. Slaves are now dressed in army fatigue gear so it is not, at first glance, easy to see who is soldier and who is slave. And then you see the welded collar and nose ring of the slave. Most slaves have paired off also and the scene is one of peace and tranquillity, which reassures you that most former slaves will settle into a new life in Europe, without difficulty.

The plane touches down smoothly on the deserted strip in Italy. There are no buildings around, but four buses at the end of the airstrip suggest to you that arrangements have been made ahead to return you to civilisation. The buses are labelled Germany, France, Italy, England, these being the places of origin of most of the slaves. Those from other countries will be dropped off en route. Germany or England? You have no idea where to go. Masters Peter and Mark are in England, you think, but Master Ian is in Germany. Your dilemma is solved when Hans walks over to you and says,

'You are to go to Master Ian's house with me. Your friend is to come too. You will travel unrestrained but when we cross the border into Germany, you will be restrained. These are the Masters' orders.'

You look at Dale and both quickly nod in agreement. Restraint at the hands of competent Masters seems a wonderful prospect, not that you were dissatisfied with your treatment over the past few months in the Sultan's palace. You bundle into the bus for Germany and four other slaves join you. They speak only German and now, a little Arabic. They are all lean and hungry looking, but happy.

Throughout the journey through northern Italy, across the Alps, Switzerland and into Germany, you talk to Hans. He tells you that your Masters have moved heaven and earth to find and rescue you. He describes the sequences leading up to your rescue and you are humbled by the expense and effort everyone has gone to. You realise that you owe an enormous debt to your Masters and those who endangered their lives to rescue you. You realise that although you are a slave, you are part of the wider Master-slave family and that it is your duty to offer everything you have to these people. That, you are determined to do.

You tell Hans of your experiences, good and bad, about the kidnapping, the enforced hauling of buggies as a pony, the work in the fields, the nightly sexual abuse and the discovery of your love for Dale. Hans, big tough guy Hans, master of war and the epitome of manliness, is quiet. Tears form in his eyes when you tell him of the sexual abuse and torture. He adds that he has never know such suffering, not from his rescues in Africa nor the Middle East, and that he hopes you will be safe back with your European Masters. Dale adds his story, his kidnapping whilst camping in France, his shipment to the desert in a coffin and all the things that happened in the desert town. As the bus moves through the Alps you realise how you have missed this society, communicating with others, albeit often through a gag, your job, and all those little activities that make this a civilised place to be. Even in slavery, in the most severely restrained positions, the most vigorous sexual abuse, you prefer to be here than anywhere else in the world. You hope Dale will think this also.

The border guards are unfazed by your welded metal collars and nose rings. They even wave the fact that nobody has any passports. Then Hans tells you they are part of his team and there will not be any problems. They will secure a British passport for Dale and yours will come from England.

The German slaves leave the bus shortly after the border and skip through the border town, never to be seen again, probably. Hans reluctantly tells you both to kneel on the floor.

'Sorry to have to do this to you both, but orders are orders. If you had been in poor condition, we were to have nursed you all the way home, but since you are so fit and healthy, you must be restrained.' He sounds apologetic and you feel sorry for him.

'Really, don't worry about it. We are very grateful to you and your men for rescuing us. You have done a great job and I am sure the people in the desert town are all the better for your efforts. Please keep us informed of what happens there. Now please do what you have to do,' you say encouragingly.

'You know.' Hans says, stroking you both on your shaven heads, 'you are two great guys. You seem so happy in your slavery. I have had a bit to do with Master Ian and his slaves and have often wanted to try it myself, as a slave. I've had this image as a tough guy for as long as I can remember, but in recent years I have mellowed and think it's now time to work through some of these feelings. I have formed a relationship with Fritz here.'

He glances over to Fritz who, overhearing the conversation, turns his head and smiles at Hans.

'Please don't tell the other guys but he's been my Master for over a year now.' Fritz nods his head slowly and knowingly. They are the only two soldiers on the bus, and the driver seems absorbed in his stereo.

'I've asked Master Ian if we can join his slave family and he agreed to a trial period. As an introduction he wants me to be bound and gagged by the time we reach his house. I will restrain you, according to his instructions, then Fritz will tie me up.'

You are completely taken by surprise by this, having been absorbed in your own situation and not paying attention to anyone else around. Dale is gob-smacked but grins and says 'I am sure you will be most welcome in any slave family.'

Hans reaches for two sets of handcuffs and deftly applies them to your wrists, behind your back. Full leather hoods, with integral pecker gags and small eye holes are strapped onto your heads, a further strap around the mouth ensuring that the gag stays put. Your elbows are strapped together, further forcing you chests forward, and a rope is attached between the back of your collars and the elbow strap, making movement of your head difficult. You are then bent over a chair and your jeans pulled down before butt plugs are inserted. Your balls are tightly bound with leather thongs and then tied to the tip of your cock so that erection is painful, if not impossible. Manacles around your ankles complete the restraint.

You are both then seated side my side on a bus seat and anchored to the seats by chains around your neck and legs. You nudge up to Dale who responds by nudging back, confirming he is enjoying this. You are encased in leather, gagged, plugged and tied to a bus seat next to your lover and returning to your Masters; what more could be better?

A further hour into the journey Fritz comes back to where you are sitting and checks your straps and ropes. He turns his attention to Hans, who is already on his knees at the back of the bus. He has removed his clothes to reveal his muscular, scarred body and pendulous cock. Fritz reaches into his bag and extracts yards of ropes and tape and a ball gag. He ties Hans' hands behind his back and his feet together. He then pushes him to the floor and proceeds to bind him in a tight hog tie, so that his feet are touching his arms. Fritz inserts the ball gag and buckles it tightly in place. A padlock ensures the gag will not be extruded. Fritz then sits back to enjoy the rest of the journey.

You recognise the outskirts of Master Ian's town, it being the same road along which you were taken when you were kidnapped, all those months ago. The bus passes through the leather quarter and you see the pole to which you were attached that fateful night. You wish you could talk to Dale and show him the sights, but maybe that time will come later. You feel comfortable and warm in your leathers and restraints and, without a hint of anxiety or apprehension, you relax in your seat.

The bus pulls up at Master Ian's house and the driver immediately gets up and leaves. His job was to drive the bus, not have anything to do with what happens on the bus, or subsequently. You notice Master Ian standing in the doorway of the house. He seems younger in the crisp evening light. He advances towards the bus then up to the two of you, casting a cursory glance at the hog-tied Hans in the back.

Master Ian reaches over and pats you both on the head. 'Welcome home boys. Now we've got work to do. Masters Mark and Peter are ready to receive you in the house and take you back to England next week, after you have recovered.'

Your hoods are removed and you are released from the bus seat and helped out of the bus and into the house. Hans is released from his hog tie but with arms still bound and gagged, he is marched into the house.

Masters Peter and Mark are sitting in the lounge room and you move towards then, one step ahead of Dale, who is not quite sure what is happening or how to behave. You kneel in front of the Masters, with your eyes cast down, and wait. Dale follows your every move.

'So, you are back at last, looking so hot in those leathers, which will have to be removed. And you, boy, we will get your clothes off too,' Master Peter says firmly, but without aggression. 'We apologize for what happened to you and we can assure you it will not happen again. The so-called Master who kidnapped you has been dealt with and, well let's say he is not inclined to take the top role any more. In fact, you will find him being traded between Masters in Germany. His sentence as a full time bound slave will keep him out of mischief for a long time.

Our job now, is to get you, both of you, rested and recovered. You will notice that Hans has joined our family, so your job will be to help him understand the role of a slave, both as a sex object and a domestic slave. Fritz here is his Master and we will teach him how to treat his slave. Any questions?'

This was truly a novel way for Master Peter to address you, actually asking for your opinion. You wondered if the whole experience had mellowed him. You hoped not.

'Sir, Dale and I are lovers. We are keen to serve you in any and every way we can, together and apart. All we ask is that we not be separated for long periods. If we are to be used by others, we wish that it be together. Sir, we are grateful for all the trouble you have taken to get us back. And we are sure the other slaves, indeed, all the people of that small desert town, are also grateful. We wish no harm for the Sultan who treated us kindly, most of the time, but the slave trader is a nasty piece of work and you can do with him as you wish. Sir, please be assured that we live to serve you.'

You had rehearsed your speech and then, having delivered it, realised it was time to shut up.

'Quite a speech boy. We agree to all those terms and look forward to having you both serve us. The Sultan will come to no harm; he will be imprisoned for 3 months, then released. The slave trader will spend at least a year in the dungeon, chained up and hopefully abused by other prisoners. After that time he will mysteriously disappear, and will be found permanently gagged and chained in someone private farm. Justice will have been served.

For now, the both of you will be released and can wash up. Shave your faces, balls and heads too. Your neck collars and nose rings will remain.

For tonight you will sleep together on the floor of our bedroom, before we start your retraining process. We don't know what you did in that place, but we want you remoulded to our tastes.'

'Yes Sir,' you answer in unison.

PART 20

Your bonds are removed and the butt plugs taken out. Once again you are naked apart from your metal neck collars, nose rings and for you, the PA. You suspect it would not be long before Dale was equipped with a PA too. You are ushered to the master bathroom, a modest timber lined affair but with a large bath in the middle. While the bath is running you shave yourselves, face and balls, and then shave each others heads. The luxury shaving soap was a contrast to the rough soap you had used before and the razor glides effortlessly over your heads, removing the fuzz that had grown. Your faces and heads glow as your lower yourselves into the hot bath.

Bath salts and bubbles create a luxurious, soothing ocean. You soap each other up, massaging the soap into holes and cracks previously ignored by regular showering. Dale's two fingers up your arse sooth the irritation that the butt plug has caused. He pummels your back and shoulders to ease away the aches and pains and you do likewise to him. You are aware that this uncommon luxury is unlikely to be repeated, so you make the most of it. You run your soapy hands over Dale's smooth, tanned body, pinching his nipples and plastering his mouth with kisses. He responds with an immediate erection and you thrust two fingers into his arse to enhance the effect. You are careful not to let him cum in the bath; that's for later, you think.

Thoroughly clean, shaved and smelling sweet, you towel each other off and move towards the master bedroom. The Masters have prepared a double mattress on the floor and a few blankets and this seems like abject luxury compared to the hard, tiled floors of the Sultan's palace. Master Peter indicates a bottle of massage oil beside the bed and as Dale lays down on his front, you pour it over him and massage his skin from head to toe, being sure to pay special attention to his arse, which surely will get lots of attention in the near future. He groans with pleasure and turns his head so you can kiss him. You turn him over onto his back and notice his huge erection.

The Masters watch from a couch and Master Mark, pointing to Dale's cock says, 'Well, do something about it.'

You lower yourself onto Dale's cock and with a few thrusts he bursts into your mouth. It feels like gallons of cum trickling down your throat, then you realise it's been weeks since either of you were allowed to cum. As you suck the final drops from Dale's cock, your hands start to massage his front. His nipples are erect and you massage them firmly. Dale winces with delight. As your hands descend his torso, he becomes erect again but you ignore it, massaging oil around his balls, between his legs and around his thighs. It seems he is screaming out to cum again but you know better than to help him without the Masters' permission.

You swap places and Dale massages the sweet smelling oil into your skin. Your erection demands similar attention and the Masters are happy to nod permission. Dale's finger finds your arse again and within a short time, fingers up arse and mouth over cock, you shoot into your lover's mouth.

The Masters are keen that you should not entirely forget that you are slaves, so attach chains to your collars, the ends of which are attached to the wall besides their bed. As you snuggle up to Dale, your bodies become one writhing, glowing, living statue of skin and tangled limbs. You kiss long and deeply. The Masters enjoy the spectacle and leave to you your own devices as they climb into bed.

Night falls and you ponder your good fortune. Chained to the man you love, at the same time a permanent slave to some of the best Masters in Europe. How lucky can you be? And you think of the future. Your job in England is still open and you don't think Dale will have any problem getting a job.

You are sure that word of your experiences will be all over the Master-slave network and people will be anxious to see you first hand. Maybe there is even a book to come out of this! For the moment though, you savour Dale's body, the memories of the past and the prospects for the future.

A Boner Book

ABOUT THE AUTHOR

Pavel Servus is a pen name and this is his first book in the BDSM genre. An Anglo-Australian now living in northern Australia, Mr Servus has travelled widely, not least being through the leather clubs, bars and baths of America and Europe. He has been on both ends of the whip and has listened to the stories of many Masters and slaves, their fantasies and fetishes. He constructed this story from his personal experiences, the stories he has heard, and a fertile imagination. Many of the scenarios described in this book will appeal to those who understand what being a slave is all about and they require no further explanation. Mr Servus offers no apology for the creative nature of the story because it does not have to be so fantastic. Everything in life is possible.

www.ingramcontent.com/pod-product-compliance
Lightning Source LLC
Chambersburg PA
CBHW051139260626
47170CB00005B/1884